Before

Before

Irini Spanidou

ALFRED A. KNOPF   NEW YORK   2007

THIS IS A BORZOI BOOK
PUBLISHED BY ALFRED A. KNOPF

Copyright © 2007 by Irini Spanidou

All rights reserved. Published in the United States by Alfred
A. Knopf, a division of Random House, Inc., New York, and
in Canada by Random House of Canada Limited, Toronto.

www.aaknopf.com

Knopf, Borzoi Books, and the colophon are registered
trademarks of Random House, Inc.

Owing to limitations of space, all permissions
to reprint previously published material may
be found at the back of the book.

Library of Congress Cataloging-in-Publication Data
Spanidou, Irini.
   Before / by Irini Spanidou. — 1st ed.
      p. cm.
   ISBN-13: 978-0-375-41381-0
   1. Young women — Fiction.   2. Nineteen seventies —
Fiction.   3. New York (N.Y.) — Fiction.   I. Title.
PS3569.P354B44 2007
813'.54 — dc22   2007005265

Manufactured in the United States of America
First Edition

Before

FEBRUARY

SoHo was dangerous then. Most buildings still housed working factories, many stood empty, and only a few had been turned into living lofts. Late into the night, pockets where new bars had sprung up were boisterous with life, light streaming out onto the street like iridescent mist and rock music blaring as one walked by. But the surrounding areas, often stretching for blocks, were all but deserted and the scattering of solitary rows of lighted windows did little to assuage a passerby's fears. Every day came new reports of robberies, muggings, a shooting or a rape. Just that week, unable to force open the police lock on the door of a loft, the robbers had taken an ax to the adjoining wall, hacking a four-by-five hole.

The eight-story building where Beatrice and Ned James lived had only two other tenants. One lived on the floor below. The other, a man named Perkins, lived on the same floor but had been in prison since before they moved in and they had never seen him. That morning, as Beatrice came out of her loft, he was standing at the opposite end of the hall, locking his door. His back was turned to her and he could not see or hear her through the loud music coming from downstairs, yet his body perceptibly stiffened.

Beatrice waited for him to turn around so she could introduce herself but when he did, no word would come out of her mouth. His eyes stayed on her with intimate persistence, and he too said nothing. In a moment, he tossed his keys up in the air, caught them in his fist, put them in his pocket — each movement deliberately slow — then he pulled the watch cap he was wearing lower down his forehead. Though he was standing close to the stairs, he waited for her to go down first then followed, keeping a steady two steps behind.

For five flights, she had no room to breathe. When she came to the ground floor, she rushed to the door and let it slam after her. Turning, she waited for him to come out so she could apologize, but all he did when he reached the door was bring his face closer to the wire-mesh window. There was a tense alacrity in the stillness of his gaze, like a sex-dark glance that blindly knows its aim, but there was no desire in it — none she could feel.

She walked away. After she had gone halfway down the block, without forethought, she turned around a second time. He had come out of the building and was standing on the sidewalk close to the door with his peacoat unbuttoned, legs apart, gently shifting his weight. He had taken his cap off and was holding it between his palms, folding it up in a roll, unfolding it, eyes down, intent on the task. He was aware she was staring — there was something too alert, too inexpressive about his face. That he had known she would stop and look back at him she was as sure.

She didn't know what he had been in prison for. All she

and Ned knew about him was his name, which was scrawled on the mailbox next to theirs with jagged characters that did not connect, in the manner a child first learns to write. Still, knowing his name had lent some substance to their thoughts about him. And they had thought about him a great deal. The two lofts were connected by double glass-paneled doors, which were blocked with an armoire on their side. The armoire did not clear the overhanging transom, and this chink in the dividing wall annulled any sense of privacy and safety that comes from a solidly delineated interior space. It was like living on a stage with the curtain always a sliver open, the seats dark and empty, and the play interminably on. Even after they had become accustomed to the situation, the silent, dreary emptiness of a place that has gone long unlived in continued to seep through from the other side.

Last night, for the first time, a light had sliced through, but the silence had remained palpably intrusive—an eerie presence their voices floated in. After they'd gone to bed, they'd heard Perkins pace endlessly back and forth. His footsteps had echoed during the night, and Beatrice had been unable to sleep. The lull when the pacing would momentarily stop had been hardest for her to bear. His presence had seemed stealthy and all the more pervasive then, and Ned's steady, rhythmic breathing had been a wall hemming her in, without giving her shelter.

Sudden, she now thought as she walked on. When something warily anticipated actually happened, it always seemed sudden—like loud thunder after lightning struck.

She was twenty-five, slender, with curly brown hair and delicate, harmonious features: high cheekbones, wide-spaced gray eyes, evenly shaped thin lips. It was not immediately apparent how strong her intelligence was; in part, because she was too beautiful to create a deeper impression; in part, because her eyes had a languor, a dreamy haze to them.

At this point she didn't know what to make of Perkins. She had an uncanny ability to form accurate first impressions — her imagination riding over intuition's gaps, if at times with too overblown a flourish — but they took time to surface in the articulate part of her mind. All she had now was a feeling about him — of fear and a murky sexual attraction — that she couldn't pry apart from a deeper, vague foreboding.

It was a Sunday and the streets, normally packed with trucks, were empty. It was like walking through a ghost town. In the bright sunshine, the buildings rose off the pavement in a shimmer of pale yellow light, their windows, opaque with years of grime and dust, glinting in the sun like dark, tinted glass. There was no one outside, no car passing by. It wasn't till she reached the narrow streets of Little Italy that there was noise — the slow traffic of a Sunday morning, people milling about. Trash cans, the sidewalks, rolled-down store gates were covered with graffiti, peace signs, and antiwar slogans. They had become a permanent part of the landscape in a way that one saw them and no longer noticed, but her eye was caught by a placard planted in the small plot around a tree like a makeshift cross marking a grave. It read, RESIST!!!

Alongside, the ground-floor window of a tenement had been set up as a shrine to a soldier killed in Vietnam. His photograph, concave and yellowed at the edges, stood between a paper flag and a statue of the Virgin Mary. It was a headshot, blown up from a much smaller picture and blurry, the face

of a man no more than twenty. Smoke from the small votive
candle had darkened the outer edges of the windowpane but
the part of the glass in front of the photograph was clear and it
seemed as if the dead man was staring out on the street, at life
as it went on without him.

Beatrice felt a pervasive sadness, his intangible presence.
*In some years, those who knew him will no longer be able to
imagine him alive,* she thought. This photograph would be all
that remained — immortalized, the sad yearning in his eyes,
his life no more than the sound of his name, the time it took
to say it.

It was early February, a clear, chilly day. Sunlight gleamed
bright around the naked branches of the trees, the twigs quiv-
ered silver-white. For a moment she had no sense of a substance bracing the life around her. If consciousness persisted
after death, the world would appear immaterial, in all its
tumult, static — just like this. *How is it real,* she thought, *this
beauty?* How was it real, walking unharmed in bright sunshine, while men were dying in the war every moment?
Often she had this feeling, of dread and numbing disbelief.
They who protested the war had righteousness and rage to
hold them up. She did not take part in protests.

As she started walking again, a black Oldsmobile drove by,
the Who blaring out the window:

> *You hold the gun and I hold the wound*
> *And we stand looking in each other's eyes*

The song resounded down the street full-blown and near,
then far and dying away. Ned had not once crossed her mind
till this moment.

◆

As Beatrice came close to Faye Knowles's building, she walked slower, with reluctance. She and Faye were childhood friends. The friendship had been foisted on them by their parents, who were themselves close friends and had forced the two girls to do everything, go everywhere together since they were toddlers. They couldn't be more different in personality and temperament, and didn't get along. Had they stayed in Illinois, where they grew up, they would have drifted apart, but here, like exiles in a foreign land, they'd held to each other fast. Even so, it was a tortuous friendship, and in the last few months the strain between them had been rapidly growing.

Beatrice wished she had not agreed to go over but walked on doggedly, believing she was bound by her word and only dimly acknowledging that she was compelled by fear. It didn't stand to reason, but intuitively she believed that everything one did in life hung together like cardboard pieces of a puzzle, and if a single piece were taken out, they would all come loose. Willing any change caused her too much anxiety. If she undid one thing, she thought, she'd have to undo them all. There'd be nothing left to hold on to. Better trapped than out on a limb alone.

After taking a deep breath, she rang the bell.

Faye opened the door and stood with her head bent back and to the side, her arms akimbo, hands on her hips. "You're late," she said.

She was barefoot and wearing only a bra and a half-slip.

Last night's mascara bled in black, viscous circles around her eyes.

"You're not dressed yet," Beatrice said, looking away.

"Getting there."

Faye walked down the long corridor, swaying her hips.

In the living room, the air was thick with stale cigarette smoke. The curtains over the windows were drawn, the silk-shaded lamps on the side tables still on from the night before. An empty wine bottle and two long-stemmed fluted glasses — one of them lying in a puddle of caked red wine — sat on the marble coffee table.

"How did it go?" Beatrice said, looking at the trail of discarded clothes that led from the couch to the bedroom door.

"It went . . . He didn't spend the night, if that's what you mean."

"Did he say anything?"

"He" was Ivan Ross, a record producer. Faye was an actress. She was starting to have some success, playing an evil seductress in As the World Turns, and had been trying to showcase her voice, with no luck as yet.

"He'll give me the show. One night, but he'll advertise."

"That's good then?"

"One night . . ."

"It's something."

"Everything's something."

Beatrice threw her coat over the Chippendale chair by the sideboard. The living room was decorated in Faye's mother's taste for opulent comfort and ostentatious grace. Except for the bedroom, which remained Faye's inviolable domain, the apartment was furnished with things chosen and paid for by her mother, and was like a microcosm of the world in which Beatrice and Faye had grown up.

"Where are we going?"

Faye lit a cigarette. "I thought we'd try Moss." Inhaling in quick short puffs, she looked at Beatrice's miniskirt and skintight, tie-dyed T-shirt, her high boots and fishnet stockings. "Don't you look hot to trot," she said, her eyes gliding over Beatrice's legs then lifting to her braless small breasts.

"Cut it out, Faye."

But Faye continued to stare at Beatrice's breasts a moment longer. "How are you doing, Trixie?" she said in a low, soft voice.

"I'm doing fine." She stressed "fine" with so much vehemence it sounded like spite.

"If you do any finer, let me know. I'll worry," Faye said, reverting to her usual sarcastic tone.

Beatrice followed her into the bedroom.

The floor here was almost impassable amidst clothes — whole outfits and dirty underwear — shoes, play scripts, copies of *Vogue* and *Harper's Bazaar*, empty shopping bags, crumpled wrapping paper and various trash. In the midst of it all lay an open overnight suitcase. It had lain there since New Year's, when Faye had flown to Saint Bart's for two days.

"What man could ever put up with this mess?"

"What man, indeed," Faye said flatly.

She was a redhead, tall, hefty, and lithe, big-breasted, large-hipped, and had a broad face with sensuous, if coarse, prominent features: a wide, full mouth, large, keen green eyes, and a flat-bridged nose. When she was alone she slumped, but in the presence of anyone, including children, she flaunted her body with flirty swagger.

"Ah, well . . ." she said after a moment of bleak, tense silence. "Let them get the neatness they need from their wives, I say."

She sat at the vanity table, cleaned up the smudges around her eyes, added fresh mascara, then got up and, staring at Beatrice, doused herself with perfume — splashing it and patting it dry, her hand slow between and under her breasts, lingering down the thighs.

"Giving myself a French bath," she said.

Beatrice sat down at the edge of the bed. On the wall behind her, hanging over the bed, was a photograph of Faye in the nude, taken by an on-and-off lover of hers named Sarah Dienst. Sarah worked large scale, solely in black and white. This particular photograph took up most of the wall. In it, Faye was reclining on her side, arm bent at the elbow, head resting on the palm of her hand. The print had been overexposed and airbrushed, so that white blurred into black as if the picture had been shot through mist. Next to it, near the end of the wall and half hidden behind the door, was a painting of Ned's, given to her in return for an unpaid loan. He had painted it two days after his grandmother died, and it was of her empty room: a straight-back wooden chair in front of a blank gray wall, a narrow window off to the side, a rectangle of sunlight on the bare floor.

"This?" Faye held a bright green sweater under her chin. "I think it brings out my eyes."

"Get on with it."

"Does it make my skin look yellow?"

"No," Beatrice said without looking at her.

"I think I'll wear black. I think I'll wear my black leather pants and that silk thing Daddy sent from Paris."

"I'm going to wait outside."

When Faye came out at last, she was wearing a sedate, beige Chanel dress and had teased and lacquered her hair into a compact pageboy, a stiff wave of side bangs covering the corner of her left eye. Rather than draping loose around her as designed, the dress filled out and stretched over her curves.

"I thought I'd be Jackie Kennedy — in a hall-of-mirrors mirror. Like?"

Beatrice put on her coat, and said nothing.

"Where did you get that?" Faye said. "A rummage sale?"

Beatrice's coat looked like a cassock, black, ankle-length, with a raised collar and a flaring skirt.

"Ned got it for me."

"What was it, a Halloween present?"

"Don't use that tone when you talk about him."

"I was not talking about him."

"Yes, you were." Her face had turned white.

"Jeez, Trix. Settle down."

"Can we go now?"

Faye took her sable coat out of the hallway closet and slung it over her right shoulder. She rode roughshod over convention but in small, surprising ways stuck to code — she would not smoke out on the street. She lit a cigarette, took a deep drag, and put it out. Sudden and jerky like a tic, a jovial smirk pulled at the corners of her mouth.

"Let the good times roll," she said.

◆

Moss was overrun with plants — hanging from the ceiling, on pedestals against the walls, in barrel-size pots interspersed on the floor. There was a lackadaisical, hippie feel to it: mismatched tables and chairs, pottery plates, patchouli-scented candles, drug-gaunt waitresses and patrons. Faye and Beatrice sat opposite each other at a table by the window overlooking Seventh Avenue. In back of them, most of the tables were empty. The few other customers — all in their early twenties, around Faye and Beatrice's age — sat slumped in their chairs, hungover and sleep-dazed. Cigarette smoke drifted in faint swirls through the stale air from the night before. Only near the window was it truly bright. Too bright. Faye had to shade her eyes with her hand.

"Know what you want?"

Beatrice stared down at the menu cover, an offset from a grainy newspaper photograph of a GI squatting on dry, cracked soil. The shadow from his helmet, which had "Love" written on it, covered his whole face. Though barely discernible, his features created an impression of meekness.

"If they really wanted to make a statement, they should have shown him with a bullet in his forehead, the helmet on his chest: Love is dead."

"Love is his name," Faye said.

"How do you know?"

"The photo is from the *Times*. I read the article."

"Yeah, well, he may have been killed by now . . . Ending up in a body bag and now here, on a piece of paper people turn over to see what there is to drink and eat. Disposable — any way you have it."

"Sarcasm doesn't suit you," Faye said, staring Beatrice hard in the face. "You should leave the sarcasm to me."

"It's the truth. You can't take anything seriously, can you?"

Sarcastic she might be, Faye thought, but her feelings ran deep even if she didn't voice them. No manner of browbeating and indignation would change a thing. She waited a moment, trying to hold her peace. "So what did you do last night?"

"Nothing — stayed at home. Ned went out drinking."

"I thought the whole thing about being married is you don't have to stay home alone Saturday night."

"Stop it!"

"What?"

"You know what. I love him."

"Wake me when it's over," Faye said.

While they were still in high school, Faye had slept with practically every boy on the football team, one of her English teachers, and her godfather, a man in his sixties. Beatrice had been the girl boys only dreamt about, too intimidated or respectful to approach her. With her looks, her willfulness, her brains, everyone back home had thought she would have the world at her feet. She had been good at any subject, talented in music, in writing, in dance. Every teacher told her she had promise and preened over her, while Faye they'd barely notice, unless she raised hell. Then, months into her freshman year at Barnard, Beatrice had gone in a single leap from virginity to free love, carried away by the time's current of rebellion and drugs. She claimed she wanted to be a poet and had written a few poems in a gushing lyrical style that showed some talent, but she lacked commitment and persistence. Outside a bad marriage and a lowly job in publishing, she had no life. With her recent success, Faye had had her small victory, and it had been a sickening pleasure watching Beatrice fall so low.

"Let's order," Beatrice said impatiently.

Faye beckoned to the waitress, a sloe-eyed, frizzy-haired blonde, leaning against the bar. A swizzle stick hung like a long toothpick from the corner of her mouth. She chomped on it a couple of times, staring straight at Beatrice then Faye, but made no sign of walking over.

"Nice slim body," Faye whispered.

"Slim?" Beatrice said, piqued. "If she's slim, what am I?"

"You're slight."

"And what are you — obese?"

"I'm put together."

Faye beckoned to the waitress again. This time, the swizzle stick no longer in her mouth, the waitress pushed herself off the bar giving it a shove with the back of her arms and walked over in a mincing high-heel teeter. There was a stoned gleam in her eyes but when she came closer, she smiled with an unexpectedly fetching smile. It made Faye sit upright.

"Bring me that lox and cream cheese what-d'you-call-it thing," she said. "And a Tanqueray on ice."

"The same."

The waitress looked at Beatrice from the corner of her eye. "The same everything?"

"Times two what I'm having," Faye said.

Beatrice pushed the menu to the center of the table. "I can speak for myself."

"That, she can," Faye said to the waitress.

The waitress lifted a loose strand of hair off her forehead with her pen. "Do I know you?" she asked Faye. "I know you from somewhere."

"Try TV."

"You're Faye Knowles!" the waitress said in a fluttery voice. "I watch the show."

"What do you know. A fan after my heart."

The waitress blushed. "I'm Sylvia," she said.

The Beatles' "Got to Get You into My Life" came on the jukebox. Drumming on the table with her hands, Faye sang along in a loud, mawkish voice.

"People are looking at you," Beatrice said.

"Don't you mean 'us'—they're looking at *us*?"

"That's a great song," the waitress said.

"You like it, Sylvia? My friend here"—and Faye pointed at Beatrice with her finger—"used to like it too."

The waitress left to get their drinks.

"I wouldn't have made her for a soap-opera person," Beatrice said.

"The plot thickens . . . Mushy by day, hot by night. I like."

Beatrice pushed back against her chair.

They were silent.

When their drinks came, Beatrice drank hers fast, immediately ordering another. That one, too, she drank fast. Faye was still on her first drink, sipping it slowly. Alcohol made her face look puckered, ashen and puffy, like she'd been soaking it in formaldehyde. *Leave it to Bea*, she thought, *to drink like a fish and never get a drunken bloat under the eyes, never lose her pink glow.*

"Chain-drinking?"

Beatrice shrugged it off. "Want my tomato?" she said, when the food came.

"I'll have your tomato," Faye said. She tore into her bagel in the greedy, slovenly way one may eat at home alone, but with aplomb, impervious majesty rising above what the populace might say. "Don't I always?"

Beatrice took the lox out of her bagel and started eating it with a fork and knife.

"Perkins . . ." she said after a while. "The man next door — the man, you know, who was in prison — he's out."

"Oh?"

"I ran into him this morning. He's older — thirty-five, thirty-seven maybe.

"He's cocky . . . dark . . . smug . . .

"There's something unctuous about him . . .

"I shouldn't have said 'unctuous.' *Sleek*. He's sleek . . .

"He's like an animal — he has no doubt who he is . . .

"He has a confident ease . . .

"He knows exactly what he wants . . .

"He has no regrets, no futile wishes . . .

"He lives the moment . . .

"He knows what's happening around him before it happens — like — like he can second-guess fate."

"Can he levitate?" Faye said. "Better yet, can he cook?"

"I'm a fool for talking to you."

Faye rolled her eyes. "All I can say is: don't!"

"Don't what?"

"What is it with you and men? He's a fucking con for Christsake. He may be a murderer. You don't know what he was in for."

"Whatever it was, he's done his time."

"Listen to you."

"I shouldn't have said a word."

Faye reached out and touched Beatrice's hand. "Can't you see I'm worried about you?"

Beatrice moved her hand away. "Don't!" she said sharply and a second later, softly, "worry, I mean."

Faye looked away.

When they were eleven, Beatrice had spent the summer at the Knowleses' house in Maine. Of that whole summer all Faye could remember was a day she had seen Beatrice ride her bike down the steep hill to the shore. She had perfect control, a concentration so strong her face was stern. She did not use the brakes. At the straightaway she leapt high in the air, landed without swerving, and glided on down the empty road. There was brightness in the air around her, of the sun, though it seemed to have been of her beauty.

Faye had waited by the roadside till enough time passed not to let on she had seen. She felt envy. Envy, indistinguishable from despair, over what she lacked and Bea had innately. Envy, indistinguishable from love — for she had desired her even then. If one could call pain love, she loved her. She had always loved her. Like a soft spot in a scar-hardened wound her love for her was, and it hurt to see her looking so lost and brittle.

In the past an air of purity, an apparent goodness, had made Beatrice seem fully, solidly herself. Now despair had picked her clean. She was still stunning, but her glow came as from a paper lantern with an exquisitely painted shade, easily torn. This change, so devastating to Faye, made Beatrice ever more appealing to a certain kind of man, who has chivalrous feelings for women and fantasies of rescue. But then, more often than not, her recent insecurity made her act aloofly and seem standoffish and elusive — hard to get, in a way that allowed men to build any fantasy about her — sadistic, in the main, as the more aloof she looked, the more her passivity showed through.

To Faye, accepting a man's chivalry was opening a can of worms. At best chivalrous men were passive-aggressive. As for sadists . . . what it came down to was a rock-and-hard-place choice: can of worms versus hornets' nest. That's what marrying an asshole got you — it paved the way for more assholes to follow. *Well, it takes two to tango,* she thought. It was hard for her to look at Bea these days without wanting to grab her by the shoulders and shake her. She was now sipping her drink with her head down, still brooding over Proud Villain Perkins no doubt.

Faye made a funnel around her mouth with her hands and yelled, "Ground control to Spaceship Trix . . ."

"That's getting stale . . ." Beatrice said.

Stale, Faye thought. So it was.

A young man with a cowboy hat pushed to the back of his head grazed their table as he went by. Beatrice shifted her weight in her chair and looked away when he winked, but her face had lit up at his glance. Though the man had moved on, she fluffed her hair self-consciously and turned her head to see where he sat.

"You were not his type — apparently," Faye said, in an offhand tone that did not quite conceal the jabbing satisfaction in her voice. She looked Beatrice in the eye. "I always say, good riddance to bad rubbish."

Beatrice reddened and lowered her eyes.

"I'm ready to leave," she said.

Faye coughed, as if to clear her throat.

"Sylvia," she said, waving the waitress over. "My friend here wants to leave. I'll have a Wild Turkey neat."

Beatrice put a twenty down on the table.

"It's my treat," Faye said.

"Take it."

Faye looked at the money and away.

"So long, Bea . . ."

After Beatrice left, Faye looked out the window and watched her as she crossed the street. Cars screeched to a halt, swerved, blasted their horns. She glided through the traffic as if she were sleepwalking. It had become windy, and her hair separated in coiling, tangled strands, flying up, swinging across her back, as wild as her pace was calm. An Antonioni frame. Better yet, Fellini — the heroine, larger than life. Black and white. The last scene . . . the opening scene . . . it could go either way. Faye could well imagine herself playing the role.

"So, Sylvie . . ." she said, when the waitress brought her the drink. "What time are you getting off?"

After two years at the Art Institute of Chicago, Ned had come to live in the city. It was a time when the influence of the New York School of painting was just past its peak and the art world was embracing the glamour of commercialism that was the latest incarnation of the American Dream: anyone could become famous and rich. A nihilistic sensationalism pervaded the work, and much of the excitement on the art scene lay in the glare of a roving spotlight: openings, uptown parties, and the elite crowd that hallowed a quick succession of bars and dance clubs, dominating social life from Manhattan's Upper to its Lower East Side. The arts had become the city's hub of energy and its foremost lure, even though a lot of it seemed like a circus — big top and sideshows, barkers and self-avowed freaks making the news every day.

He had a one-room apartment on East Twelfth near C — rent-free in exchange for taking out the garbage and cleaning the staircases once a week — and shared studio space in a cold-water flat on West Twenty-eighth, just off the flower district. Nights, he hung out at the Kettle of Fish and occasionally the

Cedar and Bradley's, where a couple of waitresses he knew sneaked him food and drinks. Once in a while he painted houses or worked loading trucks to eke out a living.

He had yet to fall in love. He tended to pick up women with an eye to where he'd find the least resistance and no fuss after. At twenty-two he thought he had life down pat: you work hard, you tell nobody your business, you don't give a sucker an even break, and you expect to get shit from the workings of fate.

One night, after he had been in New York almost two years, he fell in with a group of Max's Kansas City regulars who knew of a party and had decided to crash it. Max's was in its heyday then, and its crowd out of his league. It had taken him weeks to stake his ground there, and even after he'd broken in he was still near the cutoff periphery, an outsider looking in.

The party was at an apartment on East Tenth Street. His first sight walking in was a woman go-go dancing on a table. It was her apartment, he was told. She had a pretty face, a shapely body in a tube top and hot pants, and thalidomide-stunted arms ending in stubby hands. Her eyes were lewd with drugged-up cheer and she was bouncing her stumps with a jerky, all-out abandon that made him wonder what it'd be like to screw her. It might have to come down to that. The punch was spiked, and people were standing or milling about in stoned silence, some nodding and swaying to the blaring music, some weaving like they were about to fall off their feet.

Ned felt as one does hating a show but hesitating to leave because he's already paid for the ticket. Deciding to check out the rest of the apartment, he walked past two small

alcoves, each with a double bed in it, and came to a closed
door. He opened it. It was a large room, fronting the street.
There was little light — what came through the windows from
the streetlamps and from a few candles scattered on the
floor — but he recognized Lou Reed sitting on a windowsill
and Gerard Malanga straddling a cane chair. On a couch
against the wall sat a hulky, gray-haired man in biker gear
and, cuddling against him, Beatrice.

It wasn't love at first sight. She smiled, but it went right by
him. His mind was racing over his closeness to fame. If he
wasn't going to make history, he could at least say someday
he'd been a witness to it. He was there. Malanga, Reed — the
biker, too, looked to be somebody.

All three raised their eyes and gave him a hard, quickly
indifferent glance. Beatrice kept staring at him. He could
now feel the heat in her gaze — took in the wild curly hair,
the long bare legs.

"I'm going to move about some," she said.

She hung her bag over her shoulder, got up, and walked
out of the room with a drunken sway. Ned thought she was
making a play for him. He tended to discount the appeal of
any woman coming on to him, and her beauty — in the dim
light, a vague radiance over the shadowy planes of her face —
he saw merely as a pall weighing against his chances. Her
confidence too, the way she moved toward him, a sultry
glance gliding from his face to his crotch, put him off. It was
too dark to see the color of her eyes. She smiled at him as she
went past, and they lit up — candid with pure joy, guilelessly
trusting like a child's — which, rather than moving him, confused him.

He waited before following, to see if she'd turn her head to look back.

She didn't.

Till the party began dying down, he stood at the edge of the room, by the door, nursing a single beer just to be holding something in his hand, and watched her. She seemed to know everyone. She seemed — the way she rubbed against men, her head to the side, bending back against a kiss — at once slatternly and unsoiled. Whenever her eyes strayed to him, she gave him a beckoning smile, not quite forward, not quite coy.

In the end it was Beatrice who had made the first move. So wasted by then, she kept repeating herself, making little sense, telling him her name three times without asking for his.

"I'm Ned," he said.

"Ted . . . Where do you live?"

He told her.

"That's good," she said. "It's close by."

When he brought her home, she walked straight to the bed, took all her clothes off as if he weren't there, lay down, and passed out.

His apartment had a single, barred window opening onto the bottom of a narrow airshaft. It was early June, sweltering weather. In the morning the sparse light, like a silvery fog as it filtered through the humid air, gave a shimmer to his grimed sheets. She lay on top of them, her face tranquil with sleep, her body luminous as if the scant light in the room spilled out of her skin. He didn't want to wake her. He wished he could fuck her just as she lay, unaware of him, and it looked like he was going to get his wish: when he climbed on top of her, she didn't stir till he'd touched her between her legs. Even so, she didn't open her eyes till he'd gone in her, and then she stared at him gasping, looking confused but not scared. Seeming to recognize him, she smiled, and in a moment, pulled his head down to her and kissed him on the mouth. She was hot, moist, soft — her mouth, her cunt — moving to his rhythm, and he found himself slowing down, caught in an undertow of tenderness he'd never felt before.

She did not try to cuddle afterward. In a few moments, she asked him where the bathroom was. She got up without covering herself, went, and walked back toward the bed, looking on the floor for her clothes. He was on his second cigarette by then, taking deep drags, sitting up with a pillow propped behind his back, part of the sheet pulled across his lap.

"I have a morning class," she said. "It's my last — ever — and I'm free."

She smiled — not at him. The moment before, when she had spoken, that too had been in an aimless, floating voice like a thought uttered out loud.

As she opened the door to leave, she turned her head and looked at him. "Ah!" she said, startled as if she'd suddenly remembered something. "I'm Beatrice."

◆

Three weeks later, walking home from the apartment of a girl he had just had sex with, Ned dropped in at Stanley's, a bar up the street from where he lived. It was not a place that had anything to offer him — mostly a hangout for writers, old-line leftists, and college-dropout radicals, with too few layabout women. On that night, at past two in the morning, it was the last place on earth he wanted to be but he felt low and restless, and he was desperate for one last drink.

For days he'd been fucking a different woman every night, with Beatrice constantly on his mind, believing he'd never see her again. But there she was, sitting at the bar between two men, leaning against one and locking eyes with the other, laughing. The place was overcrowded, buzzing with noise, but their eyes met across the room at the same instant. Blushing, she slid to the center of her stool, picked up her glass, and drank what was left in it down to the ice, her head bent. He walked straight up to her and tapped her on the shoulder.

They moved in with each other that week.

Over the summer they lived in a sublet in his building. Ned worked with confidence and joy. Her faith in him and her excitement over every single painting he had done or was presently doing sometimes oppressed him, making his doubts over himself and his work seem lodged in self-hate, but he had not had anyone encourage him till then and it was inspiring to believe her praise.

She told him she wanted to be a writer but had difficulty persevering and envied his ability to give himself body and soul to his work. For his part, he saw her ambition as proceeding from sheer vanity, a dilettante's narcissistic wish to stand out without wanting to pay the price — in her case, the desire to make an even greater mark in the world than her good looks and privileged background already gave her outright.

This may have been harsh, but it was a sore point with him that the rich, who, as he thought, had everything, should want to poach in the fields of artists. Beatrice had an independent income. True, it came to a small monthly sum but it was enough to live on without her needing a job. There was a rub in that, but he kept his mouth shut about it.

For the first few months while they were happily in love, he would think back on that night at Stanley's often. In a single moment, the cynical, bitter knowledge he had of himself and of life had collapsed, and a terrifying feeling of hope had laid him open and vulnerable. He had gone up to her, though everything in him told him to run. It had been a leap of faith, and it had paid off. Later, when things started to fall apart, he would dwell on his first take on her, on his guardedness the night they first met and on the next morning — how she had left, telling him her name and not telling him her number. The truth of that first knowledge, he had come to believe, was the real ground under their feet, and her love for him and his need, a mirage they had both let themselves be blinded by. The bridge of loneliness that connected them was impassable, he thought, and like a knife in the heart. Leave it in, you die; take it out, you die.

◆

Beatrice had not graduated from college. She had passed her final exams but had deferred submitting her senior thesis to the following fall. For the first few weeks after she and Ned moved in together, she tried to work on it while Ned was at his studio space uptown. The title was *Either/Or: Søren Kierkegaard/Simone Weil.* She had hundreds of notes and, so far, only the epigraph page typed:

> The comfort of temporal existence is a precarious affair. It lets the wound grow together, although it is not yet healed, and yet the physician knows that the cure depends upon keeping the wound open. In the wish, the wound is kept open, in order that the eternal may heal it. If the wound grows together, the wish is wiped out and then eternity cannot heal it, then temporal existence has in truth bungled the illness.
>
> SØREN KIERKEGAARD

> In the period of preparation the soul loves in emptiness. It does not know whether anything real answers its love. It may believe that it knows, but to believe is not to know. Such belief does not help. The soul knows for certain only that it is hungry. The important thing is that it announces its hunger by crying. The danger is not lest the soul should doubt that there is any bread but lest, by a lie, it should persuade itself that it is not hungry. It can only persuade itself of this by lying, for the reality of its hunger is not a belief, it is a certainty.
>
> SIMONE WEIL

"Wish"/"Hunger." She saw the two as polarized: male/female, intellect/mysticism. Her end point would be connecting Weil's central idea, "Love is not consolation. It is light," and Kierkegaard's, "The truth is what ennobles."

Through her four years of college, she had read every word Kierkegaard had written, including his letters and journals, several essays on him and a biography. Simone Weil she had come to at the start of senior year and, though she had had to read most of it in French, she had read all of her work as well.

She could not proceed. Since falling in love, she had started to suspect that both their philosophies might be specious: they were built on an idea of life that denied personal intimacy and sex. Words, she thought — words, words, words . . . What was the point of adding more? She had found happiness. Had they?

This — this happiness, this love — was the reason she was born. It was what everyone sought beyond riches, beyond power, beyond fame: being one with another person, not for a moment feeling separate or alone.

She believed she and Ned had that.

The fact was she had had six months before meeting Ned to write her thesis and she had not been able to write one word, only notes — chopped sentences connected with dashes. She couldn't bring herself to put a cohesive thought into proper syntax. It wasn't that she lacked the ability. She had a stubborn resistance out of fear that the mental energy she'd have to apply would do violence to the intuitive truth, cogent, certain, and clear in her mind.

Her thesis adviser, to whom she had shown some of her notes, had told her, pressing his shoe against her shoe, "Aha!

Emily Dickinson in prose," and after she had moved her foot away: "These are spores of ideas. Unsown."

Ned, helping her set up her desk by unloading her books from a crate, had held them up as if touching them made the flesh on his hand recoil. She understood. She had cringed with embarrassment, reading the titles through his eyes: *Fear and Trembling, The Sickness unto Death, Gravity and Grace, The Concept of Dread, Waiting for God, Purity of Heart Is to Will One Thing, Concluding Unscientific Postscript . . .*

He had not said anything at all, but it had been later that same day that he had first called her Bea.

"Hey, Bea! Have you seen the hammer anywhere? I thought I'd left it on top of the fridge."

She had put the hammer away in the cupboard under the sink. She brought it over to him.

"Where are the nails?" he said. "What have you done with the fucking nails?"

He looked her in the face with mean impatience then glanced at her bare legs. There was a smutty leer in his eyes.

No man had ever been short with her before, or made her feel sluttish.

"Sorry," she said. "I put them away."

He seemed like a total stranger suddenly. He seemed like he was wearing an impenetrable mask, and, under it, she could sense only scorn and hate. She was frightened. As distant as she felt from him that moment, she felt distant from herself. It was as if nothing solid was in her and she was watching herself from someplace above, disembodied, and the only thing that seemed real was the shame he'd made her feel. She had never felt shame about her body before.

When he grabbed her, she clung to him with her arms tight around his back, kissing him with closed eyes, her tongue fighting back his darting tongue — with fear, with tenderness, with desperate want, blindly seeking the love that had been in him only minutes earlier.

She saw him clearly in time. By then they had become inseparable, and all that was base in him passed through her as pain, whose passage, deeper and deeper, numbed the surface and became the crux of her being. She knew him. Her own self she did not know. When things started to fall apart, no ground was left for her to stand on. She had given herself over to him completely. Without him, she believed, she was nothing.

On the Sunday Beatrice had been having brunch with Faye, Ned woke up at noon, sat on the sofa with a cup of coffee, and played Led Zeppelin, then Pink Floyd, with the volume all the way up to get his blood running. After a couple of hours, he still felt sluggish, and the music was merely bludgeoning his nerves, getting no rise. In a swerving turn in mood, he put on Muddy Waters.

> *She moves me, man*
> *Honey now don't know how it's done.*

The needle got stuck on "done." The syncopated rhythm of voice and scratch made the word a rasping, plaintive cry of never-ending wonder — *done . . . done . . . done.*

He lifted the tonearm and slammed his finger on the stop button. "Tell you how it's done, Jack. She makes you believe she's gonna save your life," he muttered.

With the sound of the music gone, he could hear the windowpanes rattling in the wind, and now a piercing, clattering sound came from the street. He walked over to the window to see out. The garbage cans had been toppled. Empty cartons skidded and tumbled on the sidewalk. Like confetti at parade's end, small bits of refuse swirled up and drifted in the air. In the far distance, Beatrice was walking in the middle of the empty street. Shoulders hunched, head bent to butt the wind, she staggered and swayed to stay on a straight line — intransigent, Ned thought, even in this.

Moving away from the window, he could feel the emptiness of the loft expanding into his mind. Emptiness — it was always there. It receded like a tide while he worked, then flooded its way back. An ocean of emptiness . . . staying afloat . . . drinking . . . turning on . . . bar small talk . . . fucking women on the fly . . .

It was early afternoon, the sun still strong. For all that drinking in natural light made him feel like he was going for broke in limbo, he could not resist. He went to the kitchen, filled a water glass with scotch, and gulped it down.

The second drink he nursed. When Beatrice came in, he was slumped on the couch, legs on the coffee table, arms crossed over his chest. She glanced at him and immediately lowered her eyes. Without greeting him, she hung her coat and went straight to the sink for a glass of water.

"I hate it when you shave over the dishes," she said.

"You could have washed them before you left."

She lifted the glass to her mouth and stared at him over the rim. Her eyes were lurid with liquor, her face flushed and damp with sweat.

"Where were you?"

"I had brunch with Faye."

He got up to get a beer. Better pace himself, he thought, or they'd have another row. There was only one bottle left, lying on its side on the bottom shelf. He bent down to get it. In the light from the open fridge, her thighs were aglow with black-edged pink facets where the fishnet stockings cut into her skin. Higher, like lace-frilled tourniquets, her garters made soft rings of swollen flesh. He could smell her. Reaching up, he slipped his hand between her legs. She was hot and wet. That he had to wonder whether it was from Faye or now, him, stopped his hand. He could feel his fingers turn to ice. He stood up and made to move away but she pulled him to her. She pressed against him, rubbed her breasts against him, keeping her face turned away. He didn't know how she could still arouse him so fast. Anger was part of it — she had to be piss-drunk to want him, and then she shut him out with her mouth.

"Kiss me," he said.

"I can't."

She put her hand over his prick.

"You have to use something."

Years on the pill, she opened her legs to any man she fancied — married to him, she couldn't say "condom" out loud. He took a rubber out of the watch pocket of his jeans, turned her around, and forced her to bend over the counter. He entered her violently — wouldn't let up.

Her back was still writhing as he pulled out.

"Whores don't kiss," he said.

She watched him throw the condom in the garbage pail, pick up the beer bottle from the floor, and walk to the couch, his back stiff with rage. She had straightened up, was standing with her right hand on the counter for support, her body limp and trembling. With slow movements, bringing to it a hesitant, concentrated effort like someone barely awake, she took off her boots, garters, and stockings. Bending her head, she looked down at her bare feet. Pitiful they were — high-arched, delicate, ending in crooked, crimped toes, inflamed and throbbing with pain.

My poor body . . . she thought. He'd robbed it of all joy. There was no more to be had. When he'd been passionate and tender, when he had been humble with adoring love, sex was like pouring balm on a wound in her soul she didn't know had been there till the sweet ache of its healing. Now, it was like drowning — coming up for air — and he, wanting to seal her mouth with a kiss — he, wanting her dead.

She had never been unfaithful to him, at first because she had been so passionately in love, later because the sex had become loathsome. She could still feel desire and become aroused, but her body seemed a thing separate from her, her cunt, in its moist warmth, its scent, its pulse, a small animal balled up between her legs, squirming in its captive nest.

"I'm out of fucking cigarettes," he said.

He picked a butt out of the ashtray, nipped off the burnt end, and lit it.

"So, how is Faye?"

"You don't care how she is."

Looking away, he took a long swill of beer, banged the bottle down, and put the cigarette back in his mouth.

"She's having a show in three weeks," she said, walking over. She sat down next to him. "A cabaret act. She'll be doing Gershwin."

"Gershwin! Get real."

"I take it you won't go."

"Got that right."

"I'll ask Colin," she said after a while.

Colin lived in the loft below. He composed music, painted, wrote literary criticism, and, through all that, managed to single-handedly put out *AstroNuts*, a magazine of poetry and comics. He came from Boston and lived on a trust fund. Ned had grown up in Scranton, and even when he tried to put class prejudice behind him, the name "Colin" alone caused him to sneer. Oddly though, Colin's furtive, lovelorn glances at Beatrice, whenever they ran into him, made Ned feel compassion — a wary bond, man-to-man.

"It's not Colin's scene," he said.

"I'm sure he wouldn't mind."

"I bet he wouldn't. *I* mind." He searched for another butt long enough to relight. "Colin is not a dog you can take out on a leash."

"I don't know what you're talking about."

"Yeah . . . All you know is wreak havoc in a man's life and hang him out to dry." He threw his head back, tilted the bottle straight up, and guzzled the last of the beer down. "I'm going out."

"Where?"

He didn't answer till he was by the door. "I'm going to watch the game at my brother's."

"What game?"

"The *game*," he said. "What fucking difference does it make?"

She stood up, as if better to hold her ground against his anger, but lowered her eyes. When she raised them, her face had taken on the stolid dignified expression she usually employed to thwart him.

Their relationship had come to the point where resentment and anger, triggered by the slightest and often insignificant cause, exploded full force. Ned had been wanting to leave her for a long time now but still loved her, rage tearing harsher at him than it lashed at her and making him, ever more desperately, want her. If she but opened up to him, he thought, he'd go down on his knees.

He waited for her to say something.

She said quietly, evenly, "See you later then."

He went out the door, slammed it shut behind him, then opened it again to thrust his head in and shout, "You . . . whore!"

This time he did not close the door behind him. It gaped, slowly sliding, creaking, toward the jamb.

It took all Beatrice had to take a step forward so she could close it, and then she could not move farther. Her eyes were dry but her lungs ached as if she had been sobbing—hard, the way she used to when she was three, four and punished by being sent to her room. Sadness had been an unspeakable emotion then—a pretty girl had to wear a pretty smile, same as pretty, unstained, unwrinkled dresses—and loneliness, not a word she would have known to use.

After doing the dishes and preparing the beef stew that was now simmering on the stove, Beatrice sat down to read a manuscript she had brought home.

Part of her job at the publishing house was to read manuscripts by once-prominent authors whom Carol Dyer, her boss, did not want to alienate but had peremptorily rejected because their last books had low sales and poor reviews. The task was to locate what, if anything, worked in them, so she could fill the standard rejection letter with mollifying praise. She had to "find the good," as Dyer put it. Finding the good was the sole prerogative of her job — finding the good, so that it could be used to ease the dismissal.

The mainstay of her duties for Dyer was secretarial work. When she was first hired, she had been told that an equally basic part of her job would be reading through the slush pile with a view to discovering new authors. Over three years, none she had passed on to Dyer had been published. Her letters to those authors she made personal and long, agonizing over just what to say to absolve herself of inflicting the blow. Among them were writers who were talented but lacked the ability to shape their work so as to give it a coherent vision. Lines in their books caught her breath and turning them down was like pouring weed poison over a sapling whose ripened fruit she craved. Then, there were writers who had no talent but a story to tell. If great literature was life's suffering transmuted into beauty, these books were the suffering itself. Cliché-ridden, sentimentalized, or cloaked in literary platitudes, they were nevertheless sincere, she thought. By her character, as well as by her youth, she was stubborn and idealistic. Writers who were slick, ponderous, arty, or trite she rejected blithely, even with a vindictive glee, as if smashing idols that displaced a god she worshipped. Paraphrasing Saint Paul, she believed that art made apparent things that mundane living kept unseen.

This particular manuscript bore the title *It's All a Crap Game*. A note from Dyer had been taped to the top page: "Lay it on thick—I know the author's mother. Need this back pronto."

Late afternoon light streamed through the windows but only in the studio was it really bright. In back where she was sitting, the light was the violet-gray of deepening dusk, a demarcation between the outside world and felt life. She did not mind the onset of night. Solitude was something she could lean on. But this would-be twilight, confined, as it was, to the walls of the loft, made for a loneliness that bled out into the air she breathed—out, and back in.

She started to read:

> He was on a roll. Blackjack was his game. He did not believe in luck. Luck was for losers. He counted numbers. He counted numbers and could smell the dealer's sweat. Yeah, luck was for losers. Jay Frick had his way. He could sucker-punch Lady Luck any day, and leave her begging. Never mind the goons were out to get him. If he had one belief, it was this: the only way out is deeper in. It's what you don't yet know that can save you.

She tore a small piece of paper off the pad she drafted her rejection letters on and wrote down: "The only way out is deeper in. It's what you don't yet know that can save you."

She did not keep a journal but wrote down quotations and her own thoughts on loose scraps of paper that she stored in a shoe box on the armoire's top shelf: locked-up fragments of herself—articles of belief. In the armoire, too, were all her books, organized by category, each section in alphabetical order, neatly upright on shelves Ned had built after removing the hanger-rod inside.

> Jay Frick had paid the Devil his due before, sure, but that's not the same as saying he had bedded with him. It was not easy, making his conscience take the dive — a belly flop, most likely.

> None of this would have happened if it had not been for Dolores. Answer me this, Jay Frick thought. Would you have fallen for a woman named "Sorrow" in English? What's in a name, you say? Destiny, that's what.

On a new scrap of paper, she copied: "What's in a name? Destiny." Meaning could be found in anything, anywhere — even this schlock, she thought. It was all in the way you looked at what met the eye.

"Beatrice: 'giver of joy.' "

It had been her mother's name. Her mother's — who had died in childbirth, who everyone said was beautiful, and then fell silent, as if nothing more need be added.

Giver of joy . . .

"Whore," he'd called her.

◆

Ned came home drunk around four the next morning. As he opened the door, he saw Beatrice lying in bed under a shaft of shimmering light. The rest of the loft was so densely dark that the bed appeared to be suspended in black empty space. The light's trajectory made a line up to the ceiling and across, to the transom on the far wall. Even as Ned realized that the light was coming from Perkins's side, disbelief continued to hover at the edges of his mind: the light traversed the loft at some length, hit the high ceiling at a point above the bed, deflected downward and, widening as it fell, framed Beatrice's body within parallel lines at a slant, like a painting crookedly hung. The image had the suffused brilliance of a dream: her arms rested straight along her sides, her hair flowed down her shoulders, her lips were slightly open; over and around her, the rumpled sheets glimmered like low snowdrifts in moonlight. She looked so still and serene, she could be dead.

He called out, scared: "Beatrice!"

Her eyelids fluttered.

He turned on the lamp by the door and called to her again: "Bea . . ."

It was hot. The loft was fitted with both radiators and a ceiling heater. The steam heat had just erupted, hissing through leaky valves and clanging in the pipes. The air became fetid fast, with a smell of rusty metal and mold he could taste on his tongue.

"Bea, I know you're awake."

She opened her eyes, squinting in the light. Without turning her face to look at him, she lifted her hair and pushed it up on the pillow.

"I'm sweating."

Arching her neck, she clasped her fingers on the frilled neckline of her nightgown and pulled it open.

"Why is it so hot?"

"You forgot to turn off the heater."

He unzipped his pants, staring at her breasts—a soft swell of flesh, one nipple bared, erect, the other a shadow shifting under lace. She had closed her eyes again, and at the sound of his approaching footsteps, her mouth tightened and her body turned rigid.

It was like trying to enter a squeezed fist. His loneliness was so deep he could not tell it apart from self-loathing, but he kept pounding at her. It was endless—he had had too much to drink—but he continued to thrust with insistent, dulled force, while she stayed under him breathing evenly, her face turned away.

"You didn't use anything," she said just after he came.

He moved to the edge of the bed.

Beatrice stayed where she lay, Ned's come trickling out of her, sticky and still wet on the stained sheets but already drying on the inside of her thighs, pulling and crinkling the skin. Feeling it in her and on her made her feel numb, a numbness that had the depth of despair, as when one first awakes from a nightmare, feeling still afloat on the numbness of sleep.

"Do you have those dreams," she said in a while, "where you're falling—where it's like you're weightless, drifting down like a leaf?"

"No."

"I often have them. I had one tonight."

"Doesn't sound *un*pleasant," he said.

"There's nothing to break my fall . . ."

He did not respond. In a moment he got out of bed, put his jeans and T-shirt back on, and went to the clothes tree by the door to get his cigarettes out of his coat pocket. Not finding any matches, he put a cigarette in his mouth and walked to the kitchen to light up at the stove.

Ned was a short man, prematurely bald. Broad shoulders and the intensity of his bearing made him look taller than he was. He had a high forehead, magnified by the receding hairline, a fleshy mouth with a fuller lower lip, hard blue eyes. Now, he leaned the small of his back against the counter by the stove, taking deep drags as he smoked and letting the ash lengthen and fall off; his eyes were small with exhaustion and bloodshot from alcohol, though drunkenness had drained out of him and he felt, if anything, too sober.

His workspace took up almost the whole loft, and its empty immensity made the living area look drab and confined. There was little furniture in it: a Formica-top table, disparate chairs, a sofa picked up from the street and covered with an Indian-print bedspread, a coffee table made up of a white-painted piece of plywood and four cinder blocks that formed the base. Down a wall, in a row, were a metal shower stall, a sink, a refrigerator, and the stove. The armoire, a massive piece of solid oak with trellised-flower carvings over the doors, stood at the center of that same wall.

Hundreds of paintings, done in radically different styles that reflected the Rothko, Pollock, de Kooning, and Cy Twombly phases he had gone through in the three years they had been married, were stored in stacks at the opposite end of the loft. They were dead to him, euthanized hopes — a phrase that he had coined and gave him proud pleasure to repeat. "Euthanized hopes" they may have been, yet the paintings were neatly stacked and protected from dust.

Among his friends he talked about rising above commercialism and trends, the idiosyncrasy and slow maturation of genius, the sanctity of art, van Gogh dying penniless and mad, Cézanne living a simple life far from the limelight. To himself, long ago, he had stopped the pretense. What he craved was fame — to see his name on the gossip page, to command the huge amounts of money artists were beginning to command. To be somebody.

He threw the cigarette in the sink without putting it out and lit a new one. The memory of Beatrice under the light started to splinter into transformed images: slipping between storm clouds, a faint sun ray . . . below, an altar of simple lines . . . a Doric entablature without inscription . . . Beatrice lying on it. Her left arm trailed down, her throat was arched, her head bent back, her hair flowed away from her face in soft, even waves. She was naked. Low on her belly, by the Venus mound, a small crow perched. The background was slate gray. There was no foreground.

He had it. The painting would come right at you — Beatrice's face in profile, the crow's face head-on. He would call it *Bea Illumined.* Everything about it, the figurative style, the composition, the pun in the title, the antiquated "illumined," the way the idea for it had come, as if decreed by fate, had charge.

It was like a floodgate had opened. Images kept rushing his mind:

A faceless woman with legs wide open, the genitals glaring . . .

Low tide — like a desert of wet sand . . .

A stormy sky, the sun like a lump of coal — a jagged black hole in a vortex of muted gray light . . .

Boundless sea, a piece of rotten wood flotsam bopping on choppy waves . . .

The back view of a man, midstride, stooped shoulders, limp hands; an alley cat prancing, its tail up; a drop of blood on flagstone; like a funnel, in distorted perspective, a comic-strip view of Gotham; night light, black granite; lighted windows, bright orange like holes in a pumpkin . . .

Eve. Like tumbleweed on an open palm, a red apple in her raised hand; a worm basking in the hollow of a tooth-marked bite; caked mud, clay-colored, over her feet and calves; the shadow of a tree in full leaf, the tree itself off frame . . .

He hadn't done figurative work since he first came to New York. He couldn't count the turns his painting had taken so far. Always, a "new" turn — *the* turn. This was a leap, if a turn back to the point at which he had first started. He didn't know why he had needed to paint then. It hadn't been about ambition. It hadn't been about measuring himself against anyone else. It hadn't been about wanting to give meaning to his life. Though at moments joy ran through him as effort dissolved and his hand moved with a surety of purpose that was purely instinctive, it hadn't been about experiencing joy. He painted — just did, like a bird sings — becoming insensible to everything around him. He could not even hear his name called, unless someone stood close and shouted at him, as if he were in a state of shock that allowed his life to go on, making for acceptance of what was un-acceptable in it.

Life was shit and you had to wade through it with no nicks on your skin — what he had believed. His work had been the one grassy knoll. Nothing had mattered beyond the moment.

Lacking high aspirations had enabled him to go unscathed through life. He'd been sure of himself, had been able to take the blows. Unhappiness used to run through him leaving no trace — same mud stirs up in the pit of a murky well, whether you throw in a big stone or small.

Enter Beatrice. Love.

She had forced the gates of Paradise open, had made him believe a man like him could enter. Hope had drained the water, parched the mud from the well, and rocks that fell in scraped and scarred the pit. Despair could have done no better.

She had forced the gates of Paradise open, then blocked the way with her body, daring him to enter — go through, like there was no flesh to her.

It had to be lovemaking or he had to fuck her cold like a whore.

Maybe she was good as gold, but pure gold was shapeless and soft, impossible to grasp tight.

A man liked some toughness in a woman, someone you could bang and hear shout, someone you could fuck and not feel you were sinking in a black hole.

She was laying him to waste.

Her unhappiness sucked oxygen out of his lungs.

Her passivity was poisoning him.

Prim like a hothouse rose — even the thorns were for show.

Beautiful, gifted Beatrice. What had she done in her life?

An idea in the head was a turd in the hand, unless you had the guts to act on it.

She had marked him from the start: the fall guy — sold him on love and laid the failure of her life on him.

Supported him! Cut off his legs and bought him crutches. He poured himself a drink and had a sip.

The sun had come up. Though the light inside was still tinged with gray, he could see it was already bright outside. In the patch of hazy sky visible from where he was standing, streaks of pink shone so bright their color seemed to be refracted through motes of crystal.

No, he didn't want a drink.

He walked to the studio and did a first sketch of *Bea Illumined*, adding or refining details as he drew. Beatrice now had larger breasts, fuller lips, less chin. The callow, graceful curves of her features and limbs were engorged to convey sensual bliss. Down the blank face of the altar ran a web of fracture lines, hair-thin and blurry like blotted ink. The crow had a white worm in its beak, a red thread around its leg, and a tag from it that spelled AS IT FLIES in cramped cursive script.

When he was done, it was in the crow that, pen stroke by pen stroke, his pulse fervently beat. The lines of Beatrice's figure, he saw, were glib.

Hey! Hey, you!"

Beatrice was startled. She had been walking with her head bent, looking at her shadow and past it, flat and gray, at the prostitutes' shadows. Now that she looked up, she could see they were not women but teenage girls. Most of them stood in groups of three or four. The one who had called out stood by herself, staking her own turf. In the freezing cold, she was in hot pants, platform shoes, sheer tights, and a fake fur jacket that barely came to her waist.

"You're about to lose your earring," she said, pointing to the crook of her neck. "On your collar."

Beatrice picked up the earring off her coat and clipped it back on.

"Thanks."

"Yeah . . ." the girl said. She took a cigarette out of the pack in her jacket pocket and lit it, taking a deep breath, a sound like a sigh. Her fingers were bloodless, pale and stiff from the cold, her lips chapped raw; gashes of torn skin gaped over thick layers of red lipstick.

"You should get your ears pierced. Wear your diamonds for real!"

After two puffs, she threw the cigarette on the ground and squashed it with her shoe. A dozen butts were scattered by her feet. She could be no more than fourteen, and the harsh makeup on her face gave off a patina of false ripeness like wax on early-picked fruit.

"I wish it'd hurry up and snow already," she said.

She had large, silver hoop earrings on, and the pierced hole in her left ear was swollen with pus blisters.

Beatrice looked at the girl's infected ear and turned her eyes sharply away.

"Thank you so much," she said.

She tried to smile, but as her lips began pulling apart the girl turned her face away with sudden, snubbing disdain.

Beatrice walked on, feeling chafed.

The sky was overcast with dense, dark clouds, in sharp contrast to the pink effulgence from the neon signs of the porn movie houses and peepshows that lined Eighth Avenue just north of Forty-second Street. The snow would look pink as it fell, she imagined — pink on the ground, like cotton candy, matching the girl's pink faux fur. Lick me . . . eat me . . . the summoning mouth frozen in a puffy curl, a horrid grin.

You should get your ears pierced . . .

She was fine wearing clip-ons, thank you. They hurt when they were too tight and were prone to give you a headache, but there it ended. She'd rather suffer the pain than have permanent holes in her ears — anything that indelibly marked her body . . . Faye had her ears pierced in junior high, in defiance of her parents. Self-mutilation — the rite of passage to independence . . .

She wondered if the girl did something for the infection.

Probably not. Yet she'd worried that a perfect stranger might lose an earring.

What had her life been like before she ended up on the street? No one chose their childhood, or the parents to whom they were born. The seed in the parable that fell by the wayside was the same good seed that, falling on fertile ground, flourished. The Lord, who later would not tear up the tares for fear of uprooting, along with them, a few stalks of wheat, let what the wind swept away perish.

And I? she thought. *I am the seed that fell by a tare.*

No. I chose to marry Ned.

Drug addicts stood sullenly in the darkened doorways of SROs. Solitary men lingered outside the sex shops or walked on by with stooped shoulders. Traffic was slow and there was little sound other than that of the few passing cars. The surrounding silence was as if the coming snow was already falling, the heavy humid air a transparency like vaporous slush. With her hair up and her face aglow with makeup, Beatrice stood out like a stray high note in a dirge, but she was unaware of it. Her thoughts were still on the girl.

Wear your diamonds for real . . .

Cryptic advice? Let your light shine?

No. The tone had been supercilious rebuke.

If you got it, flaunt it. That was more like it.

She walked at a slower pace, resisting each step forward though forward she was determined to go on. It was hard for her to walk without wobbling. Despite predictions of a snowstorm, she had worn narrow-toe shoes with tall high heels. The irony that her shiny pumps and the girl's scruffy platforms served the same end was not lost on her, but she did not dwell on the thought.

Turning the corner on the next block was a leap from squalor to riches. Dominic's, where Faye was having her show, had a gray and black striped awning, twin revamped gas lamps on each side of the entrance, and a discreet sign embossed on the glass of the door. The varnished wainscoting, brand-new brass fixtures, shellacked oak tables, and polished hardwood floor shed an antiseptic shine into the haze of cigarette smoke. Crimson velvet drapes covered the windows and, saloon style, a fan hung on a long cord from the center of the ceiling. The place reeked of fake, and Beatrice had to give up the hope-against-hope that the show would be anything more than a vanity performance.

It was crowded, at any rate. The only free seat she could find was at the bar. She recognized several faces in the back room, actors and actresses Faye had worked with, art patrons, producers, the glamorous friends Faye zealously kept to herself. Feeling out of place, outclassed — her little black dress was five years old and fell to the knee, out of style — Beatrice sat on the bar stool, back straight, arms at her sides, hands flat and tense over her thighs.

A man in his fifties got up from the other end of the bar, walked down, and stood behind her, two steps to the side. Though his hair was still dark and thick, the skin on his face sagged and folded under the cheeks, and he had deep, dark hollows around his eyes. There was an arrogance to him, a suave manner that hinted at contempt.

"Your earring is about to fall off," he said.

She hadn't noticed him earlier, nor was she aware of his presence now, and his voice startled her. She turned around, her hand going up reflexively to her right ear. *Again!* she thought.

"The other one."

Saying, "May I?" he sat down next to her and smiled.

Looking away, Beatrice took both earrings off and put them in her purse.

"You give up easily," he said.

"Hardly."

"Beatrice, I believe?" he said in a moment. "I'm a friend of Faye's. Faye told me you'd be here."

"How did you know it was me?"

"Faye said you'd be the most beautiful woman in the room."

"Yeah," she said in a cutting voice, "that's me all right."

She looked pointedly away and beckoned to the bartender to come over.

"A margarita. Salt. No ice."

He ordered a dry martini.

Beatrice turned her back to him, sliding sidewise on her seat in the direction of the empty stage in the back room. He repulsed her, but his connection to Faye made her too curious. When her drink came, she turned toward him again and, after taking a long sip, said, "So how do you know Faye?"

"Faye and I go way back."

She studied him — the rumpled well-made suit, the loosened chic tie.

"Coming from a trip," he said.

She blushed.

"You blush easily."

"Do I?" The flat, withering tone of her voice had, nonetheless, a thrust of intimacy.

She downed the rest of her drink. "You know my name," she said, motioning to the bartender to bring her a new one. "I don't know yours."

"I'm Simon Berg."

Faye had never mentioned him, not that she often mentioned the names of men she slept with.

"You have a saturnine nature," he said.

" 'Saturnine' . . . Now, that's a word one uses in conversation a lot."

He took the jab in stride. "Smile for me," he said.

She smiled with a rigor of affected sweetness and looked him in the eyes.

"How's that?"

She turned her back to him again. When her new drink came, she drank it fast, hoping the alcohol would build a moat of numbness around her. Even with her back turned, she could feel him — all the stronger feel him.

Years ago, she would have been able to shrug him off or go with him, as she pleased. She used to give herself to men easily and freely. She hadn't known what love was then. She hadn't known the beauty of her soul, hadn't known that there was something pure to sully. Till Ned her body had seemed like a gift she could bestow at no personal cost. It made men happy. It gave them so much pleasure her own was dwarfed. They made her come, and it was like jolting to a stop after a hard run — a short gasp then the slight embarrassment of being in bed with a man she didn't know.

"As always, late," Simon said.

Faye had come onstage. In a platinum wig, strapless turquoise sequin dress, all curves and undulating verve, sly sultry eyes, and cynical smile, she sang "I Got Rhythm," strutting and sashaying, a cross between Peggy Lee and Mae West.

Barely listening, Beatrice thought of Faye when she was young: the fat, pudgy-cheeked child, lazy and obstinate, bad-tempered when crossed; the bubbling laughter and teasing eyes, a woman's voluptuous body at fourteen; her messiness and wild pleasure at eating sweets, her scatterbrained enthusiasm over what piqued her interest, her habit of wearing elastic bands around her wrists, doubled so that they pressed into the skin to help her remember things; sitting with her arms around bent legs, chin on the knees, talking about boys; her moodiness, her bursts of rage, the seething sarcasm, the meanness; the promiscuity, the three abortions before she was eighteen.

They had gone together to Maine a week before Beatrice married Ned. A long farewell. Not much to say. Stayed up drinking all night the last night. Walked to the shore. Watched a small boat sail away, so far out it was invisible, its wake.

Faye was now singing "Someone to Watch Over Me," blaring out the notes torch-singer style, and it was hard for Beatrice to listen without feeling embarrassed. Even so, the melody and lyrics cut through her full force and were bringing tears to her eyes. Ned and she had watched over each other . . . early on . . . When they used to make love, it had been like they were brother and sister, so tender it was — the joy of it, like a more and more wonderful surprise after being told to shut one's eyes.

"Want a hankie?" Simon said.

She dabbed her tears and shook her head.

"I'm not really sentimental," she said.

"No, not really. You lack irony, merely." His tone was blunt and unwaveringly certain. "Not sentimental. Romantic. Sentimentality goes with cynicism. It's the cynic's thorn in the flesh. Romanticism goes with self-pity."

She looked away.

"Another drink?"

She nodded.

Simon beckoned to the bartender to bring them another round and edged closer to her. It looked like he was about to lean over, and she sat up straighter to deflect him.

"I want to listen to Faye."

"I can see that," he said, arching his brows in mockery. "You're all ears."

She bristled with anger at the taunt and blushed at the same time, for he'd seen through her unease and lack of interest in Faye's performance. When the bartender came, she took her new drink from his hand and had three long sips without taking the glass off her lips.

"You push life away," he said.

"I'm trying to push *you* away."

He smiled. She could feel his breath, hot and bristling, on her bare arm. She could feel him down to the soles of her feet. He had taken his tie off and unbuttoned the top four buttons of his shirt, revealing a small triangular tuft of scraggly hair over flabby skin. With a startling ache, she thought of Ned's strong chest — the bristling thicket of hair over his heart a prickle of softness, a prickle of warmth. Tears welled up again, and she finished her drink trying to keep them down. These days he had sex with her just to get off, and it was like he was spitting on the ground to affirm contempt. It had gotten so she wanted him to fuck her for the peace of knowing there was no lower place for her to sink.

"Whatever it is can't be that bad," Simon said. He put his left arm over her shoulders and clasped his left hand over her upper arm, giving a squeeze. "It never is. Trust me." Loosening his grip, he rubbed the tips of his fingers in soft circles over her skin but pulled away when he felt her freeze. Nevertheless, he continued to lean over. "I bet he's young, whoever it is. You should be with an older man who could appreciate who you are . . ."

She looked him in the eye. "Is that right?"

She should fuck him. She should let him have her, let him give her pleasure, and refuse in any way to touch him, leave his bed without saying a word. He wanted her body, her body he'd get. *Whore* . . . Indeed. But if vengeance, there would be no victory to it. Her anger carried such vile, violent contempt for him it would be hard to act on it without feeling debased — more, she thought, than he might feel.

It scared and horrified her to be thinking and feeling this way. She ordered a new drink, drank it fast, and, before she had quite finished it, beckoned to the bartender to bring her another one.

Moments later, a long time — she couldn't tell — there was a movement just below her line of vision, an energy felt. The bartender had come and gone, and in front of her was a fresh drink. The music had stopped, and Faye was off the stage, kissing and glad-handing friends who jostled in a throng around her. Beatrice tried to get her attention, waving her arm, but Faye did not see her.

"Want to go up to her and fawn?" Simon said. "Or are we staying for the second set?"

He had said "we" the way one says "we," coaxing a child. She turned her back to him again, though nothing seemed to daunt him. There was, again, that odd sensation of time slowing down to take a sudden leap. The bartender had put an

Ella Fitzgerald tape on and with the first bar of the music she
was back to real time.

> *Evening shadows make me blue*
> *When each weary day is through*
> *How I long to be with you*
> *My Happiness . . .*

She sang along in a whisper, swaying to the beat.

> *A million years it seems*
> *Have gone by since we shared our dreams*
> *But I'll hold you again*
> *There'll be no blue memories then*

She had danced to that song with Ned. Early on. Before the
words had felt meaning, before their sadness had a savor
other than the soothing, aching melancholy of a slow waltz
tune.

"Like I said: romantic."

"It's a song," she said. "Words flying in the wind."

"That, you don't believe."

She didn't know what she believed anymore.

She finished her drink and lifted her coat off the stool.

"Ready to flee?"

She walked out, without looking back.

The shuddering chill from being suddenly outside sobered
her some, though she could barely stand. It had not started
snowing yet, but the air was more humid and slightly warmer.
Snowflakes would be coming down any moment. As she
was thinking that her best chances for getting a cab would
be on Eighth Avenue, she had the strange sensation that she
was being stared at. She was still standing under the awning.

When she had looked up and down the length of the street a moment earlier, she had seen no one lurking. But he must have been there all along: a boy — fifteen, sixteen — sitting on the stoop stairs of the building across the street. She could not see his face clearly in the dark, only his sulky demeanor and that, dimly. He wore cowboy boots, tight jeans, a tattered leather jacket, and leaned back, legs sprawled, elbows resting on the step above. In a moment he got up and walked down the street toward Eighth Avenue, in the same direction she was about to take. He reached the corner, crossed over to her side of the street, and stood a few feet away from the street-lamp, near the curb.

His hair was parted in the middle, fell down to his shoulders, and was brown, with a copper sheen that softened the darkness of his skin. He had an oval face with sunken, dark eyes, high cheekbones, a straight nose, and slender, perfectly shaped lips. He was ravishingly beautiful — and knew it, Beatrice thought.

Feeling her eyes on him, he turned his face and stared back. His pupils were dilated and glazed, yet softened as he looked at her, and his face lost the arrogance she thought she'd seen there before. Sudden, heartrending pity brought on second sight: it was an act, the swagger; he was desperate, beaten down, scared — only a boy, and already ravaged by life.

She was too drunk to know she was describing herself, except for a feeling of familiarity and confusion, like she knew him from somewhere. She wanted to put her arms around him. But he'd turned his face away and was scanning the traffic.

She assumed he was waiting for a taxi. When she saw that

he let one pass without raising his arm, she stepped off the curb and hailed the next one coming. After it stopped, she turned around and said to him, "You aren't waiting for a cab, right?"

Instead of answering, he walked past her to the cab and opened the door for her.

She wanted to thank him but her mind was going in and out of focus again. She was already in the cab. She was pressing her face against the window. The glass was foggy. She pulled back and brushed a clear swath with her hand. He had not moved from the curb. The taxi, too, was not moving. She glanced at the traffic light and saw it was red. Vaguely, in the periphery of her vision, she saw a man in a peacoat, a watch cap pulled low over his brow. He was walking down the street in a slow loping gait, his eyes steadfast on the boy.

It all happened too fast: the light changed; the cabdriver jerked the shift into gear; the car lurched and sped down the middle lane. It wasn't till the cab idled at a second red light and she was telling the cabdriver she had changed her mind and he should take her to the bar where Ned hung out every night that she realized the man in the peacoat had been Perkins.

◆

Late at night, only the upstairs space, where there were tables and booths, was busy. The cavernous ground floor was all but deserted, looking like a way station long after the last train is gone. Everything seemed still: the purple haze of cigarette smoke, the handful of men stooped over drinks along the bar, the bartender with a cigarette hanging from his lips. Beatrice glided in as if weightless on her hurting feet and stood a ways in from the door, slowly unbuttoning her coat. Otis Redding was singing "Sittin' on the Dock of the Bay." A woman in a spiked dog collar and miniskirt was leaning against the jukebox swaying her hips a steady two seconds off the beat. She glanced at Beatrice, then with sullen indifference looked away.

"What can I do you for?" the bartender said.

She had moved but could not remember taking the steps. She was standing with her hands on the rounded edge of the bar. The bartender was leaning forward, close to her face. He had a tattoo on his forearm, of a sword with a rosebush twig winding from the tip of the blade to the hilt, bright red buds like drops of blood poking through black leaves. The song had ended. There was complete silence, then a loud ping, as a man's cue stick hit the lamp that hung over the pool table. The lamp swung back and forth on its long cord, and its light shifted across the bar like a roving beam from a searchlight.

"Bea!"

"Colin?"

How could she not have seen him? He was standing three steps away from her.

"Bea . . ." he said again.

He was a tall man, thin and lanky, with a narrow face, sad, earnest eyes, a wispy beard, and long limp hair tied in a ponytail. Invariably, as tonight, he wore a black leather vest over gauzy, wide-sleeved shirts with no collar, cutting an unprepossessing, listless figure that belied his high intelligence and deep, feeling nature.

Beatrice watched him put a cigarette in his mouth. His hand was trembling too hard to light it, and the match burned his fingers. He tried again, looking nervously at the stairway leading upstairs.

"Have you seen Ned?"

"I think I saw him leave. Yeah, I saw him leave." Hesitancy wavered in his eyes. "He went to another bar."

"You're lying."

He shook his head, but did not look her in the eye.

"Which bar?"

"I don't know which bar. You should go home. Why don't you let me take you home?"

"I know you're lying. I know he's upstairs. I know it. I know what he does."

She turned toward the stairs.

"Don't!" he said, reaching out with his arm to stop her. "What's the point?"

She pushed his arm away. She did not know what the point was. There was no point. In anything, no point — in pain, no point. She did not know why she had come. Yes, she did. She wanted to see with her eyes what she had already, many times, seen in her mind.

At first she thought she might be wrong. He was not among his friends at the large table by the landing. Then, she saw the two empty chairs next to each other, the two mugs with beer still in them.

—Bea!

—Come sit down, Bea.

—Ned's in the bathroom.

—He's in the bathroom.

—You look like a million dollars, Bea.

—He'll be right back. Come sit down.

—I'll go get you a drink.

—You want a drink, Bea?

Their faces blurred. She wanted to answer but they had been speaking too fast and now they had all fallen silent. They were staring past her.

She felt him before she could see him. He was coming toward her — right behind him, a woman with reddish hair. Her lips were swollen, smeared with lipstick. She had freckles like mud spots on her flushed skin. She was older. She had big breasts. She was wearing wide, silver, stoneless rings on every finger. She had square-cut nails varnished pearl white. She was smoothing her blouse into the waistband of her jeans.

Beatrice could not take her eyes off her.

"What are you doing here?" Ned said. "What are you *doing* here?"

He grabbed her shoulder, extending his arm, a gesture hesitant as if adrift between holding her and pushing her away.

She tried to shake her shoulder free. "Let go."

"What do you want me to say?"

"Let go of me. Say nothing."

He did not try to stop her when she turned to leave. He did not go after her, when she went down the stairs. Her footsteps echoing like distant drumming in her ears, she walked past Colin. She saw him and did not see him. He was there, not there.

Colin wanted to speak, he wanted to hold her — *solace her*, he thought, just that — but the anxiety behind the impulse was overwhelming, forcing him to own that he wanted more.

It had begun to snow, and the snow was coming down steadily and fast like a thick drizzle. By the time Colin went after Beatrice at last, her blurry figure was a blot widening into the fainter aura of its stain. He could barely see her.

He ran after her, calling out, "Bea! Bea, wait!"

She stopped but did not turn around till he was just behind her.

"Colin . . ." she said. There was snow on her face. Her eyelashes sparkled, a wet rim of tears and motes of ice. "It's you . . ."

"Are you all right?"

"I'm fine. Really . . ."

She turned her back to him and walked on.

Colin watched. He stood frozen in the blanketing snow — inside, burning.

When Beatrice woke up next morning, the space next to her on the bed was empty. She did not have to look up and see to know that Ned was lying awake on the couch. She could feel him, could feel his rage. Wading through a vision-blurring hangover, she washed, dressed, put makeup on her face, filled the percolator with coffee and water, and set it on the stove. Time seemed to run at a dead-interval pace — moments when her mind was utterly blank.

She had walked by the couch three times — on her way to the shower and back, then on her way to the stove — and each time Ned had averted his eyes. Walking by him once again, she picked up his clothes, which lay scattered on the floor where he had dropped them, and folded them neatly over the back of a chair.

"Are you getting up?" she said. "Should I pour you some coffee?"

He did not answer. In a moment he staggered up from the couch and sat down on the chair where she had folded his clothes. It was the nearest one. The clothes dug into his back and he shoved them off.

Beatrice picked them up from the floor again and laid them on another chair.

"Do you want a muffin?"

"Do I look like I want a fucking muffin?"

He reached for his cigarette pack and put a cigarette in his mouth. His temples were throbbing.

"You should have something to eat."

She set the coffeepot dead center on the table, dead center on the trivet, and walked back to the kitchen. When she came back, she was carrying two place mats and two bone-china saucers and cups, part of a tea set that had been a wedding gift from a cousin. The cigarette was hanging down from Ned's mouth, the ash breaking off. She pushed the ashtray on the table closer to him and sat at the edge of her seat, back straight, eyes down.

"It may snow again," she said, holding her cup up in her hand. She lifted it to her lips and took a sip. "There's that look to the sky."

He stared at her, smoking the cigarette with short consecutive puffs straight to the end, without taking it out of his mouth.

"Are you going to say something?" he said.

"There's nothing to say."

"Nothing to say." He banged his hands on the table, making the ashtray topple onto the floor. "Fucking shit!"

"What do you want from me?"

"For once, for *once*, I want you to show me what you really feel. *You* — I want *you*!"

"You have me."

He laughed, a bitter, cackling laugh.

She finished her coffee and dabbed her lips with a napkin.

"I have to go, or I'll be late for work."

"Oh, we mustn't have that," he said, squeezing his cup in his fist. His forearm was shaking.

She reached to take the cup from his hand. "It will break."

"Get away."

"You'll hurt your hand."

He threw the cup on the floor with such force, it scattered into tiny pieces.

"Go away!"

Her knees buckled as she tried to get up, and she had to hold on to the table so she wouldn't fall.

"It's Cyril's birthday," she said quietly. "Don't forget dinner tonight."

Her knees kept giving way. It was hard to keep her balance, but she felt calm, and when she was out on the street, her steps became steady. It was as if nothing had happened. She walked in a straight line to the subway, her eyes straying randomly around her: paw prints and a patch of urine like crystallized yellow paint on the snow; the newsstand, shuttered down; a trash can like a gigantic ice-cream cone; the bus-stop shelter, empty. It wasn't till she was inside the subway car that she started to come apart. Her whole body was shaking. Her hands, icy from the cold, were sweating. She was sure the tunnel would cave in. The train's rattling, rushing speed made time seem to run at an inversely slow pace and the distance lengthen rather than decrease. She felt trapped. It was hard to breathe.

When she was back out on the street, the anxiety attack was gone. Again, it was like nothing had happened. Traffic on Lexington Avenue was thinner; snow crested on car roofs and tree branches and piled on the sidewalk in shoveled compact masses with narrow footpaths winding through. Other than the effects of the snowstorm, it felt like any other workday.

The nausea did not come over her till she had got closer to her office building. She barely made it up the elevator and down the long corridor to the bathroom in time. After she threw up, she rinsed her mouth and splashed cold water on her face. She was afraid to look in the mirror.

In July she was going to be twenty-six, which she saw as the beginning of decline. She was young enough to believe herself old, but, more than that, her mother had died at nineteen, and having already had a longer life made her feel old. Her mother's death also made her feel great guilt. She had felt guilty too when she was small, believing she had caused her mother's death — killing her by being born — but the guilt now, of having outlived her, was deeper, if harder to articulate, and made her feel she had no right to her life.

She had latched onto Ned's love with the desperation of a loveless child. The first time they kissed had been the first time she felt love in her mouth. That was what love was like, she had thought — the love she had been denied and every-one else had known at their mother's breast. People had always thought her strong. When she was young, her strength had come out of determination alone. If there was no one to fend for her and protect her, she'd have to do it herself. She had come to that realization when she was only four.

Who am I? she thought.

When she was younger and had thought she knew who she was, what had made her feel sure of herself had been her intelligence and will—no real sense of self at all. No, the only time in her life when she'd felt complete in herself, fully alive, had been when Ned and she had been in love. Happiness had given meaning not only to her life but the world. If that happiness had but lasted, it would have been enough to live for.

What did she have to live for now?

If love didn't last, if love wasn't true, nothing could justify life, she thought.

Her need to believe in love, gainsaid by her experience, was leading her to mistrust her senses. Her life had taken on the intensity and double consciousness of dreams, where one is powerless to interfere in the course of events, where one observes what is unfolding without questioning cause and effect, and feelings are felt more vibrantly than in wakefulness yet seem unreal. Nothing felt real.

Vomiting—*that* had felt real.

She rinsed her mouth again and walked out of the bathroom, thankful no one had been there to see her.

Her office was a windowless anteroom to Dyer's office. The walls were lined with wooden bookcases and, at the far end, metal shelving that held manuscripts in several stages—read, unread, accepted for publication, copyedited, in loose and bound galleys, pages—arranged in neat, orderly piles. There was a typing table and a desk, a leather sofa where people who came in to see Dyer could wait.

She sat down at her desk without taking off her coat.

Mrs. Callaway, the receptionist, came in.

"Are you cold?"

"No . . . yes," Beatrice said, looking down at her coat.

Mrs. Callaway stood two steps in from the doorway, holding an immense bouquet of white lilies, purple irises, red dahlias, mauve peonies, and small yellow roses, arranged in a profusion of baby's breath. Dyer received flowers regularly from her authors and, sometimes, agents she worked with, and it was Mrs. Callaway who always brought them in, laying them down wordlessly on Beatrice's desk and leaving right away. She was a matronly, brisk-mannered woman who acted put-upon, having to fetch and carry. Now, there was a quizzical, forbearing smile on her face.

"They are for you," she said.

"For me!"

Her heart pounded. She took the flowers from Mrs. Callaway and buried her face in them. The bouquet was so large her arms couldn't go all the way around it.

"Someone loves you a lot," Mrs. Callaway said.

Beatrice set the flowers down on her desk, picked up the envelope attached to them, and held it in her hand, waiting for Mrs. Callaway to leave before she read it.

Mrs. Callaway lingered.

"Your anniversary?" she asked.

"No . . . yes," Beatrice said, stressing the *yes* emphatically, if anxiously, and blushing for the lie.

"Well," Mrs. Callaway said sternly, "if you forgot, he didn't."

She left, though not before adding, "I wish *my* husband bought me flowers."

The handwriting on the envelope was not Ned's. It must be the florist's, Beatrice thought. She was startled to see that the enclosed note was typewritten and had no greeting.

Your idea of love is just that, an idea.

You are stubborn.

You wear your beauty like a crown of thorns.

You do not believe you are vain. Be it said that masochism is inverted vanity, you are, indeed, most vain.

You flee to conquer. Better to stoop.

Love is a crick in the genitals, jolting the heart.

SIMON BERG

She crumpled the note in her fist.

"What's the matter with you?" Dyer said. "You look like you've seen a ghost."

She had just walked in and, like Mrs. Callaway, stood in the doorway. Her attention leapt to the flowers.

"Who sent them?"

Beatrice hid the note in her coat pocket.

"There was no note."

"No note! I have enough on my mind without having to play guessing games."

She went into her office, hung up her coat, and came back out carrying a vase. She was in her sixties, a tall, gawky woman with a frosty, impatient manner, small eyes, and a large, long-toothed mouth that made her look lewd on the rare occasion she smiled.

"Whoever it was, must have cost him a pretty penny," she said.

Beatrice reached out to take the vase from her hands.

"I'll do it," Dyer said. "I have to go to the loo anyway."

When she came back, Beatrice was sitting at her desk, still in her coat.

"Are you cold?"

Beatrice took off her coat and hung it on the hook behind the door.

"Are you sick, Bea?" Dyer said.

She walked past Beatrice, without waiting for an answer, and went into her office to put down the vase. There was no empty surface large enough. Annoyed, she placed it on a stack of books on the floor by the window, and sat down at her desk. It was cluttered with piles of manuscripts, letters to read, letters to sign, review clippings, copies of *Publishers Weekly*, interoffice memos, odds and ends that had at one time been in her purse: a pair of nail clippers, a pocket flashlight, parking tickets, half-empty packets of Kleenex, a tattered leather-bound address book, LifeSaver rolls, a key ring, loose change. Heaving a sigh, she picked up the neat stack of phone messages from the day before that Beatrice had left square in the middle of the desk. Each slip of paper had small arrows at the end and a circled "over." They would put a court stenographer to shame. Never mind how many times she had told her: name, number, reason for call—one sentence. She skimmed the messages and pushed them pell-mell aside.

"Beatrice!" she shouted. "What is this?"

Beatrice came in.

"Who is Michael Burns?" Dyer said, holding up a letter Beatrice had written and typed for her to sign.

"He's just come back from Vietnam. A reporter. He wants to write a novel about his experience there."

"'Wouldn't a novel be gilding the wound?'" Her voice dropped a notch and slowed down with sarcasm over "gilding the wound," but she did not raise her eyes. "'From your clips,

I see that you have a clear, hard eye for truth and the courage to tell it. America needs to know the truth about the war. Why not a nonfiction book? Why not the bare truth?'"

Beatrice was silent.

"The bare truth hasn't made anybody richer," Dyer said evenly. "What paper does he work for?"

"He's freelance."

"Let me see his clips."

Beatrice came back with a folder where she'd filed the clips, but instead of handing it over, she stopped midstride in the middle of the room, her eyes on Simon's flowers. In direct sunlight, petals and leaves shimmered so bright it was as if they were exhaling quivering breaths of colored light. Even as she was moved by it, the beauty of the flowers caused a chill of repugnancy in her, and it made her sick looking at them.

"Are you all right, Bea?" Dyer said.

Beatrice handed her the clips.

"Are you . . . pregnant?"

Beatrice had had a short period — just two days — since the one time she could have conceived, and no sex since. Still, the swelling in her breasts had not gone down, which gave her a queasy feeling of apprehension.

"No. What makes you say that?"

"Forget it."

It had been her volatile moods. Something about the soft puffiness of her face, the slow, heavier walk.

"I see Reg Spears called. You should get going on his book."

"It's next on my list."

"Your *list* . . . You put Spears down on your *list*!"

Reginald Spears had never been seriously reviewed, but

his books sold in the millions around the world. He wrote ponderous gothic novels with aging, gloomy, yet randy male heroes, prone to soul-searching. He was Dyer's greatest success.

"Do it now."

Beatrice went back to her office, took the galleys of Spears's book from the shelf, and set them on her desk. She had to transfer author's corrections from his proofs onto the master set. It was a job that someone in production would normally handle, but Spears demanded that Beatrice do it, and what Spears wanted, Spears got. The novel was eight hundred pages long, and he had made massive changes throughout, not excepting the title, *The Iron Castle*, which had been crossed out with an arrow pointing to an appended note.

My Dear Beatrice:

Which of the following, alternate, titles do you like best?
1. *Hell's Dungeon*
2. *Cold Was the Hangman's Hand*
3. *Night Mist*
4. *Call Me Dante* (double allusion — *Moby-Dick, Inferno*)
5. *Beatrice Awaits in Vain* (pertinence to your famous namesake and secret homage to you, whose beauty has been a bright beacon through my dark toil)
6. *Beatrice Abandoned* (ditto, above)

I favor *Beatrice Awaits in Vain*. There is no "Beatrice" character in the book, nor are there allusions to "Paradise," and that's precisely the point.

Let's discuss this over lunch. Lutèce? Monday next?

What about, Beatrice thought, shaking with hysterical laughter, *what about* Nine Circles Down, None to Go? Each time she lowered her eyes back to the note, she laughed again, and couldn't stop.

There was a postscript, written much later in a drunken hand. It sprawled down the page and over the back in a side-winding, uneven column:

> I only gave "unto Caesar" till — in the twilight of my life — I met you, my Beatrice, my dear. This is my masterpiece. I SHALL prevail, even if critics continue to ignore me. *Vox populi, vox dei* (*vide* Shakespeare). Don't think me arrogant. I stand humble before you. Beauty before genius, my lovely. Beauty before age, my love.
>
> Lutèce??? Please say yes!

Spears was seventy-three, short, with a large head and a florid face, pudgy small hands and a distended stomach, a hard-living, pugnacious elf of a man whose bald head barely reached her shoulders. Bypassing Dyer, he went over his edited manuscripts with Beatrice in person, having her go to his house, where he inevitably received her in a golden brocade dressing gown, offered her caviar and champagne, and, while they sat side by side on a sofa, repeatedly, salaciously touched her knee. She tried not to mind. The passion behind the ideas in his books was utterly sincere. His lechery was sincere. His pretentiousness was sincere. He stood just this side of ridicule with feisty, daunting poise. One had to admire that, she thought.

It took her all morning and most of the afternoon to finish the job. Less than an hour was left before it would be time to leave. She started to type the rejection letters she had drafted earlier in the week. *Promising work . . . full of promise . . . poignant with promise . . .* As she was typing the fifth letter, her mind started drifting, sinking into depression. She could be writing these letters to herself. What did it mean to have promise? All it came down to in the end was *many are called but few are chosen.*

Colin was standing on the corner of Sixth Avenue and Eighth Street, waiting for the light to change, when he saw Beatrice on the opposite side of the street, head bent, back bent, a Balducci's shopping bag in each hand. She was walking as if her legs were barely holding her up, and he leapt through traffic to help her.

"Colin . . . It's like you're following me," she said. She burst out laughing. "You look like the abominable snowman."

He was wearing a hooded down jacket, padded mittens,

and enormous fleece-lined galoshes. The hood had a rabbit-fur border that came down to his eyebrows and a snap-on flap that covered the lower part of his face.

"Sorry," she said, trying to catch her breath. "Sorry—I don't mean to laugh. What are you doing here?"

"I'm coming from my shrink. His office is on Ninth Street."

She started to laugh again, a whimpering, moaning laughter.

He waited for her to stop.

"Want to have a drink? I always have a drink after I see my shrink."

"Washes down the advice?"

"Washes down something. He doesn't give advice. Repeats to me what I say."

"That's funny," she said, no longer laughing, not smiling.

"Yeah. It wouldn't be half as funny, if I weren't paying him big money."

He picked up the shopping bags and led the way to McBell's.

"Just one drink," she said.

The bar was almost empty. They sat at a table in back, hiding in plain sight.

"I'll have an Irish coffee," Beatrice said to the waiter.

"Good idea," Colin said. "The same for me."

Beatrice lowered her eyes. "About last night . . . I want to thank you." She raised her eyes but as they met Colin's, she exploded in hysterical laughter again.

"Are you all right, Bea?"

"I don't know," she said. "I don't know what's come over me. I could kill myself the way I'm feeling this moment."

"Don't say that."

"Right. I'll just keep laughing."

The waiter brought their drinks, and they drank in silence.

"Colin," Beatrice said offhandedly after a moment, "how would you take it if a man sent you flowers with an insulting note?"

"Insulting — insulting how?"

She took Simon's crumpled note out of her coat pocket and gave it to him to read.

"You threaten him in some way," he said. "I don't think his intention was to insult you. Show he has power over you. Maybe."

"Power over me . . . He despises me, I think."

"Why would anyone despise you, Bea?"

Like an oar's shadow over water, a dark gleam floated in her eyes.

Colin stared at her covertly.

He was by nature a solitary, reserved man. He had been an only child, reclusive and high-strung. Knowing he'd never have to worry about making a living, his parents had encouraged in him an interest in the arts and given him a free hand to play an open field. His talents were limited, and he knew it: he was a servant, where there was a plenitude of masters, but he was as the good and faithful servant to whom the Lord had given two talents and who had earned Him another two — *faithful over a few things, ruler over many.*

Till Beatrice, desire had never preyed strongly on his emotions, and even with her his feelings were less sexual than romantic. Still, he couldn't stop thinking about her. Though his mind reeled from imagining her naked, he masturbated thinking of her. He looked at other women thinking of her.

He worked thinking of her. When he was not thinking of her, he sank into depression till he started thinking of her again and desire bounced him back to the belief that in the end she'd love him.

"You have beautiful eyes," he said.

"Don't I." She gave him a tight, self-scorning smile and drank down what remained of her drink.

They were silent again.

"I have to get home," Beatrice said, when she was done with her drink. "Cyril is coming over for dinner. Do you know Ned's brother Cyril?"

"You brought him to my party."

Colin remembered Cyril too well: he had spent almost the whole night talking to Beatrice, slumping over her with possessive lustful ease. The word was he had been to Vietnam, was doing construction work, did dope, and sometimes dealt.

"That's right—you've met him," she said, getting up. "It's his birthday . . . Some celebration that will be. I barely slept last night." She passed her fingers through her hair. "Do I look awful?"

"You could never look awful."

She turned her back to him. He could see her shoulder blades quake, as if he had touched her with an icy hand.

She walked toward the door. "I'll wait for you outside."

Colin stood up abruptly, knocking down his chair. "Your coat!"

She walked back.

"Don't know where my head is . . ."

Long legs, skinny arms, tall neck, narrow head, like a stick figure in a child's drawing, Colin bobbed and weaved as he searched his pockets — the back, front pockets of his jeans, the small pockets in his vest — coming up with crumpled bills, his face stern with the effort to regain dignity.

Beatrice looked away, her arm frozen midair toward her coat. Slowly she let it drop, startled to realize he was shy — so big and forthright a man. She had always thought of him only as a friend, and being moved by him now made her edgy. Avoiding his eyes, she touched his arm to ease his nervousness but he shunned her hand, pulling vehemently away. He picked up the shopping bags off the floor and, rigid, his face tight, walked past her and out the door as if they had just had a fight. It took her a moment to follow. When she walked outside, he was standing at the curb, scanning the traffic for a cab.

"Would you like to come to the dinner?" she said in a curt voice, standing a few steps behind him. "It will be Cyril and Ned — and me."

He didn't answer. She walked closer and touched his sleeve.

"I heard you, Bea."

"I want you — to come," she said. "Please, come."

"What would I be, the fourth wheel?"

He stopped a taxi and opened the door for her.

She hesitated.

"Get in!" he said.

He put the bags next to her on the seat, squeezed in on the other side and gave the driver the address. The car rolled slowly down the icy street. Colin looked out the window. The piles of snow and flattened slush were a misty purple-gray in the gathering dusk: the view through a telescope, the universe in a single gaze. *Near*, he thought, *and far away.*

He wanted to touch her. He wanted to touch her, and his arm lay rigid, tight at his side, like a prosthesis whose mechanism he couldn't work.

He turned his face from the window and sat upright, looking straight ahead.

"Colin, are you mad at me?" she said.

◈

It was understandable how his imagination had taken a leap from Beatrice sleeping on white sheets to Beatrice lying on a marble altar, but the crow? Ned had known next to nothing about crows. Expressions: "eat crow"; "as the crow flies," which he had used; "crow's feet." He had observed crows in nature, though no more curiously than other birds. The small knowledge he had garnered came by looking through *Birds of the New and Old World*, as he searched for a photograph of a crow to paint from. Crows, he had learned, could modulate their cawing to imitate the human voice. They fed on dead flesh. They made good pets. Of all birds, they possessed more intelligence than would be sufficient for them to survive. The same was true of man — what accounted for human evolution and the development of civilization, he thought. There had to be a connection between a surfeit of intelligence and emotion, a surfeit of intelligence and self-awareness . . . loneliness . . . One did not perceive animals as lonely, except for ones intelligent enough to be tamed. Did loneliness preexist their attachment to man — was it inextricable from responsiveness to love?

In the book on Delphi, where he found the daguerreotype on which he had based the altar, he had read that, to this day, crows descended from flocks that fed on the carcasses of animals burned in sacrifice circle over the ancient ruins and sometimes alight on the abandoned altars where they perch like "mourners." The story was apocryphal, no doubt. Still, of all the other facts he had culled, it was the one that had most powerfully seized his mind. In the land of tragedy, the people *would* think "mourners." No, not mourners, he thought. Faithful sentinels. Circling over, perching, in the belief the fires would light up again.

He cleaned his hands with a rag soaked in turpentine.

No pet crow, his crow. It had a sullen dignity and, for all its small stature and minute purchase on Beatrice's body, it stood with a conqueror's staunch stance. The crow had come off, he thought. It captured the essence of a crow, the uncruel rapacity in the eyes. Beatrice's figure was botched — a trite fluidity of lines — though that in itself said something, did something. It made a statement of some kind. He tried to make himself believe that, to stave off defeat, but deep down he knew Beatrice's figure put the lie to the whole composition.

He walked to the sink to wash his hands. He was about to dry them, when the door opened and Beatrice walked in, with Colin following a few steps behind.

"We ran into each other," she said.

He stared at her. "Hey, man," he said, without taking his eyes off her.

Colin greeted him with a nod. He unzipped his coat but made no motion to take it off.

Beatrice turned her back to them and started taking the

groceries out of the bags. "I can't convince him to stay for dinner," she said.

"Stay," Ned said. "Why not stay? . . . Come look at this. What do you think? I just finished it."

They walked side by side to the studio, Ned watching Colin blush as he recognized Beatrice in the woman's naked figure.

"I thought I was going to call it *Bea Illumined*," he said. "Now I'm thinking *Corvus*. Maybe just *Crow*."

"I'd go with *Crow*."

"So, are you staying?" Beatrice asked, walking over.

Colin took off his coat. She took it from him and went to hang it by the door. He followed her, without commenting on Ned's work.

"There's beer, scotch, and wine," she said.

"Beer."

She took a tall can of Bud from the fridge and handed it to him.

"More where that came from."

She poured herself a scotch and left the bottle uncapped on the counter.

"You two talk," she said. "I'll be too busy here."

She took a sip of scotch and started peeling potatoes, plopping them in a basin of cold water. Colin sat down on the couch, all the way to the side near the armrest, and guzzled down his beer. Ned sat down at the other end.

"Bea, get me a can."

She brought one over and set it down on the coffee table.

"You look like strangers in some waiting room," she said. "A doctor's office. Put on some music."

"Why don't we all clap our hands and sing?" Ned said.

"I think I should leave," Colin said.

"Leave?" Ned said, without looking at him. "The party has not even started yet."

Beatrice took off her shoes and the gray cardigan she'd worn at work, pulled her shirttail free from the waistband of her skirt, and let down her hair.

"Now I can breathe," she said, going back to the sink. "Cyril should be here any minute."

A moment after she spoke, there was a knock on the door. But it wasn't Cyril. Faye burst in, holding two bottles of champagne up high. She had on the platinum wig from the night before and was wearing false lashes, glossy scarlet lipstick, and spike heels.

"What?" she said, seeing Ned's startled, unwelcoming expression. "Cyril invited me."

She put the bottles down on the table and threw her coat over a chair. Her skintight, silver-thread knit dress showed the lines of her bra and panties and fell just below her crotch.

"Someone died?"

Beatrice was chopping onions for the chicken stuffing. She turned her head over her shoulder, onion tears rolling down her cheeks. "You were great last night. I meant to call this morning."

"Meant to call. That's a relief to know."

"I did try to catch your eye."

"I'm sure you knocked yourself out."

Faye made a beeline for Colin.

"Hi, Colin."

Colin got up but did not offer his hand and sat back down, looking away. Ned too stared away from her.

"That's new," she said, pointing to the painting. "It looks nothing like your other work." She went into the studio to have a closer look. "It's like a Magritte," she said, coming back. "Something about the colors and the imagery, something about the stilted manner. I like it. I love Magritte."

She picked up one of the bottles of champagne.

"Open it for me," she said to Ned.

"Shouldn't we wait for Cyril?" Beatrice said.

"We need a rehearsal," Faye said. "Get the birthday feeling right."

Ned popped the cork. She took the bottle from his hand and drank straight from it, tilting her head back, looking at him from the corner of her eye—a look that said, "Remember?" She had blown him not too long ago, in a dark bedroom, light coming from the corridor through the open door. She had followed him in from the partying crowd and had stood silently behind him as he searched for his coat among the pile on the bed. He knew she was there, he knew she had followed him, and when he turned around with a new pack of cigarettes in his hand, he did not move away but stared her straight in the eye, tearing the cellophane wrap off the pack. As she went down on her knees, he put a cigarette in his mouth. It had remained dangling at the edge of his lips.

"Can I talk to you?" Beatrice said.

Faye walked up to her and stood behind her by the sink. She took another swig of champagne from the bottle.

"You had no business giving him my address."

"Who?"

"You know who," Beatrice said in a low, angry voice. "Simon."

"I didn't give him your address. I told him where you worked."

"He sent me flowers."

"He does that," Faye said and, after a long pause, "He likes you."

"Right."

"He's the Berg of Berg and Gramsci. They're opening a SoHo gallery. You should ask him to come see Ned's work."

"Right."

"You never know."

"Right."

"Stop saying 'right' all the time."

"Right." Beatrice dabbed her fingers on a dishtowel. "Pour me some more scotch," she said. "I don't want to touch the bottle and get onion smell on it." She reached again for the knife. "And put on some music, will you?"

"What do you want to hear?"

"I don't care. Turn it up loud."

Faye put on Nico, *Chelsea Girl*.

Now that it's time
Now that the hour hand has landed at the end
Now that it's real
Now that the dreams have given all they had to lend
I want to know
Do I stay or do I go
And maybe try another time . . .

Beatrice wished she could close her eyes and have it all go away — close her eyes and never open them again. But she had to chop the celery. She had to dice some bread and dry it in the oven. She had forgotten to buy packaged stuffing. She had forgotten to buy salad things. She had forgotten to buy candles. The chocolate mud cake, that she had taken out of its box and set on top of the icebox, was melting out of shape. It was hot, stifling hot. No one spoke. Even through the blasting music, she could hear the silence in the other side of the room.

> *I've been out walking*
> *I don't do too much talking these days*
> *These days*
> *These days I seem to think a lot*
> *About the things that I forgot to do*
> *And all the times I had the chance to . . .*

She turned around and saw that Ned was now sitting at the table, Faye next to Colin on the couch. They were all staring at her.

❖

Cyril arrived over two hours late. He had a heavyset body, lumbering with incipient violence, a strikingly handsome, tough face. He was much taller than Ned and had a stronger presence, though Ned, with his subtler intensity and broody bearing, could be said to be more intriguing. He had brought two young girls along, who hung about him with stoned blithe confidence, unfazed by being in an unfamiliar place.

"This is Minnie," he said. "That is Mary."

It was a one-sided introduction, for none of them bothered to say their names.

The girls looked with overt curiosity from face to face then walked about with a mellow, jaded air of street savvy, checking out the loft.

"There isn't going to be enough food," Beatrice said. She was leaning the small of her back against the counter by the sink, sipping scotch out of the bottle. She had been drinking steadily since she finished cooking. The bottle was nearly empty.

Ned, who had gotten up to answer the door, was still standing. Colin and Faye sat silently on the sofa, each nestling a beer can in their lap.

"I'm in the money," Cyril said, walking up to Beatrice. "I'm flush. I can take us all out."

He took a wad of money out of his pocket. Beatrice saw that the knuckles of his right hand were bruised. There was an open gash on his thumb.

"How did you get that?"

"Hit a wall."

"It looks bad."

"You should have seen how the wall looked," Cyril said, but without humor in his voice.

He took the bottle from her and had a swill. He had intelligent eyes that were hard with smoldering rage and seemed to judge without admitting doubt. Looking at her, as he drank, a gleam of pain came to their surface, giving them sudden, jarring depth. The rest of his face showed no emotion.

"Save some for a rainy day," he said, putting the bottle back on the counter.

"It *is* a rainy day."

"It doesn't have to be this way," he whispered.

"Right."

Beatrice staggered past him and sat down at the table. "That's for you," she said to him, pointing to the champagne bottle. "From Faye. Who wants some? Warm champagne, anyone?"

"It will chill fast," Faye said. "Where's the wine bucket?"

"We have no wine bucket," Beatrice said. "Furthermore, we have no ice. We're neat-whiskey drinkers in this house."

"We can put it outside the window — in the snow," Minnie said.

"You do that," Faye said. "This one too, while you're at it." She lifted the bottle she had opened earlier from the floor and handed it to Minnie.

Faye hated champagne: it made her dizzy without making her high. The bottles were from more than a dozen sent to her with flowers last night for the show. The bouncer had helped her load them into a cab, and her doorman had unloaded them and carried them up. She had not put the flowers in water. Did not know why she had brought them home. Rounded up the show, she guessed — her DOA performance. She should have laid them over and around her on the bed, should have slept under them.

"It should take no more than a few minutes," Minnie said. "It's better than a freezer."

Faye looked at the girl — Minnie/Mary, whatever her name was — and smiled, making eyes. M/M did not catch the ball. Red paisley bandanna, laborer of free love. Not quite free, Faye bet. A round dark mole at the edge of her mouth, punctuation point to the sensuality of her lips. The other one in a

floral cotton granny dress, laced tall boots. Cyril . . . like min-
ion bodyguards they hung around him when he came in.
Pissing in the wind — and he knew it.

She got up and sat at the table, three empty seats down
from Ned.

Cyril unhooked the mirror that hung over the sink. Patches
of mold and rust were embedded in the glass, running
through it like an outbreak of mange.

"How can you see in this thing?" he said.

He set the mirror down in front of him on the table and
emptied a heap of cocaine from its white paper packet, picking up what specks remained with the tip of his finger.

They did lines, all but Colin, who sat on the couch,
watching.

"That your painting?" Mary asked Ned, pointing to the studio with a nod of her head. "I love the blackbird in it."

"It's a raven, stupid," Minnie said.

"It's a crow," Ned said.

Mary stood up. She raised her arms over her head, clasped
her hands, and stretched her sides — left, right.

"I'll put on some music," she said.

She looked through the record stacks.

"Wow. You've got some real good stuff."

She took her time to decide, balancing mood against
nuances of taste.

"Put on the Supremes," Faye said. "You can't go wrong
with Diana Ross."

The music shook the air like an explosion.

Ooh baby love, my baby love . . .

"Turn it down," Beatrice said.

Mary lowered the volume, but only slightly.

"Cocaine is the only true aphrodisiac known to man," Minnie said, doing another line.

"Known to woman," Faye said. "Men can't get it up on it."

"I don't know about that," Cyril said.

"Colin will tell you," Faye said. "Isn't that right, Colin?"

Colin walked to the fridge and took out another Bud. He peeled off the small tongue of aluminum and raised the can to his mouth. It looked like he was about to say something, but he took a sip, put down the can, and stayed silent, standing by the sink.

"Aphrodisiacs are a myth," Ned said. "There are no aphrodisiacs."

"There is — one," Beatrice said. "Love . . ."

"Love lasts two months — the kind of love you're talking," Minnie said.

"What are you — seventeen?" Faye asked.

"Nineteen."

"*True* love lasts always," Beatrice said.

Everyone stared at her.

"Yes, it does," Colin said, looking at Beatrice, then lowering his eyes. "*True* love."

Beatrice smiled at him then turned her face to Ned. "One man who agrees with me," she said in an icy, scoffing voice.

"Make that two," Cyril said. He looked at Beatrice, then, as Colin had done, lowered his eyes.

There was a long, tense silence.

"Does that painting mean something?" Minnie asked Ned. "I mean, is it supposed to say something?"

Colin cleared his throat.

From oriole to crow, note the decline
In music. Crow is realist. But, then,
Oriole, also, may be realist.

He declaimed the lines in a clear loud voice, mumbled, "Wallace Stevens," under his breath, and walked out of the loft with slow steps and his head bent.

"Is he always like that?" Minnie asked.

"Yeah. That's Colin," Faye said. "Is anyone else smelling smoke?"

"Must be the food," Beatrice said.

She trudged to the kitchen and opened the oven door. The chicken had shriveled to a charred carcass and the potatoes looked like shiny unfired coal.

"What we've been waiting for," she said, laying the roasting pan down on the table.

"I said I wanted to take us all out," Cyril said.

"You all go," Beatrice said.

Minnie and Mary put on their coats.

"Come on, Bea," Cyril said. "Fresh air will do you good."

"Fresh air . . ." she said. "I'd rather put my head in the oven."

"You had too much to drink."

"Right." She looked at him till he had to lower his eyes.

"Go, man," Ned said. "I'll speak to you tomorrow."

"Faye," Cyril said. "You coming?"

Faye put her arms around his neck. "Birthday boy," she said. "How is it—two is company, three an orgy, four a feast?"

He pushed her off. "Coming or staying?"

"Going," she said. "Not *coming*."

She headed for the door. Minnie and Mary were already out in the hall.

Cyril was staring at Beatrice, making no move to leave. Beatrice avoided his eyes. Ned watched them both, drinking fast, without taking the can away from his mouth.

"So," Beatrice said, meeting Cyril's eyes. "Happy birthday! I didn't want it to fall in a crack."

"It does fall in a crack," Cyril said.

He was born on February 29 and that day was the 28th. It wasn't a leap year.

"It's just a number," she said. "It's the idea that counts."

They were looking in each other's eyes, solemn and tense, as if confessing intimate thoughts through coded words. Watching them, Ned felt his suppressed anger rise and quiver on his skin like goose bumps.

"They're waiting for me . . ." Cyril said.

He left, without a parting glance at Ned.

"You should have gone with them," Beatrice said, when the door closed.

Ned crumpled the beer can in his fist.

"Not to worry. I'm going for good," he said, trying to steady his voice. "I'm leaving the field."

"What's that supposed to mean?"

She was standing five, six feet away from him. If she were closer, he knew he'd hit her. He went to get another beer — walk it off.

"Colin, Faye . . . my own brother," he said, coming back.

"I haven't done anything with anyone. You're no one to talk."

"What I do means nothing."

"A whole lot of nothing."

"A stiff prick has no conscience."

"You should put that on your forehead — in red letters."

Slowly, provocatively, she took her clothes off, letting them drop to the floor.

"Here," she said, looking him in the eyes. "The nothing you like."

Ned tried to resist the urge.

"We need to talk," he said.

"What for?"

"We need to talk."

She stepped up to him and put her left hand around his neck, her right on his chest, sliding it downward.

He pushed her away — roughly, though sudden tenderness made him feel sick to his stomach — and he knew, knew with sudden, absolute certainty just at that moment, that he *was* going to leave her. He might still love her, but it was over.

He said again, "We need to talk."

She turned her back to him, walked to the bed, and lay down on her back over the covers. It was the last time, he thought, walking over. It would be the last time. He slid down on her, and she opened her legs, raising her pelvis to his mouth. She was wet. She touched her fingers softly on his hair. The muscles in her belly heaved, were throbbing. He thought she had come with a single lick of his tongue but when he raised his head, he saw she was sobbing.

MARCH

Well past midnight, after leaving the party for Cyril's birthday, Colin went to score some pot from Dickie, his old college roommate. He had left his hooded down jacket upstairs, and the only other winter jacket he had was a fleece-lined barn coat. He put it on and wrapped a wool scarf around his neck, but he could not find a hat. A few minutes after he was out on the street, it began snowing again. Hudson Street was deserted. Once in a while, a car rolled slowly by and disappeared down the road. It would be a lark if he could find a cab but he kept hoping. In the meantime, he started walking toward the East Village. The snow was heavy, but it was not in his character not to go through with something once he had made up his mind to do it. Numb and aching from the cold, continually having to shake off the snow that was piling on his head, he kept on.

He arrived over half an hour later, drenched, frozen to the bone, and banged repeatedly, ever more loudly on the door.

Dickie answered at his own good time.

"Don't you own a cap, man?" he said.

The apartment was a studio — one small room with no

furniture in it, except for a twin mattress on the floor, a phone-wire spool pilfered off the street to serve as a table, and a beanbag chair. Jimi Hendrix was playing, turned low. No electric lights were on. Rows of candles burned on the windowsills and near the sideboard along the opposite wall.

A party was going on but it was beginning to die down. The dozen or so people there — four crammed on the mattress, the rest sprawled on the bare floor — nodded silently when he said hello. They all had familiar faces but the only one he recognized for certain was Dora. She had lived with Dickie for a year after college in a cabin up in Maine. That was when Dickie fancied himself a mystic. Did his noncelibate, acidhead Thoreau thing.

"Remember Albert?" Dickie said.

Bertie . . . Colin thought. He had dropped out of Yale sophomore year. Crew-cut, button-down prissy. Now, his hair and beard stood on end in tangled tufts.

"Gateway, you haven't changed a bit, man," he said to Colin. "You're like some painting in the attic."

"He was born old," Dora said.

She did not smile or look up. She sat as if cast in stone, arms around bent legs, her chin in the cleft between her knees.

"Where have you been hiding yourself?" Colin asked.

"Under a rock."

He sat down on the floor, resting his head and back against the wall.

"Watch it, man!" Bertie said. "You're ruining the fucking poster, man. Your hair is wet."

Colin looked behind him, at a copy of the Bobby Seale

poster in which he's sitting in a cobra-head wicker chair, holding a rifle in one hand and a spear in the other. Colin's hair had left a large wet stain between the feet.

"Looks like he's pissing his pants, man."

"Not likely," Colin said.

"Black power, yeah . . ."

"Right on."

Colin looked at their wan, wasted white faces. They and Bobby Seale, he thought—peas in a pod . . . The wall across was plastered with photographs from *Life* and covers from *Ramparts*, *Rolling Stone*, and *Mother Jones*: naked napalmed children, flag-covered coffins, peace rallies, Kent State, a kneeling Vietnamese man with a gun pointed at his head just before it went off—a collage of the war that the government said was not a war. He took a toke of the joint being passed around and shut his eyes.

He was six-four. Everything about his body was wispy, slender, and long: his limbs, his fingers, his toes, his nose. His legs reached to the middle of the floor. He took up a lot of space and felt as if he were taking up no space at all.

"I know you," the girl sitting cross-legged next to him said. "You're in that band—what's it called?"

"Hard Does It."

"Yeah . . ."

She had a pretty oval face, blond hair parted in the middle and falling to her waist, honey-brown eyes, and a fleshy mouth with a sharp-peaked Cupid's bow somewhat marred by buckteeth.

"I write their music."

"You used to play with them. I saw you play."

"Not anymore. I don't have the personality for it."

"You cut out?"

"I write the songs for them," he said. "I write the songs . . ."

She unfolded her legs and moved closer to him. She put her hand on his thigh, near the crotch.

"You don't remember me, do you?"

He nodded — could be "Yes, I don't," could be "Yes, I do."

She was older than he had at first thought. He could now see, under the warm glow of the candlelight, the pasty pallor of her skin, the sagging corners around her mouth. He wondered if she'd sucked his cock. There had been number-less, faceless women, and the band had not even made it big yet. He felt oddly detached from that part of his life, as if it had not been him in the flesh but his body, in effigy, fuck-ing. He had no sense memory of the sex. Even moments after, he had no sense memory of it, though a vague guilt stuck.

"Wan' a lude?"

She held up two pills on her palm; took one, washing it down with tequila straight out of the bottle. She closed her fist over the second pill — opened it, closed it, opened it.

"Want it?"

She slipped her other hand farther down inside his thigh, pressed on him. Colin had made it on Quaaludes once, and the woman had seemed to levitate weightless under him. It had been like swimming, mouth open, underwater — breathing as before birth. He did not want. He did not want. He had no want. Did not want a hard-on. Not want. Beatrice was a spreading ache in his body. He took the Quaalude to make him want — maybe want. The girl's hand felt soft on him. She had delicate hands, a child's hands. She was small. She had not told him her name. He did not want to know it. No name. No talk.

"Hey, Richard!" she shouted. "Hey, Richard! Do you have that damn record on repeat? My mind's warping."

Dickie gave her the finger.

"You look peaked, man," he said to Colin. "You look like something the cat dragged in."

The girl got up and walked to the stereo console. She put on the Doors.

"Looks like two feet of snow out there," she said, looking out the window. "It's coming down hard. Maybe you people should be leaving."

"Never fails," Dora said. "February is always a shitty month."

"It's March," Bertie said. He took a chain watch out of his leather-vest pocket. "As of an hour and forty minutes ago, it's March."

Everyone had gotten up to leave. They put on their coats, weaving.

"You'll have to let me crash," Colin said.

Dickie just looked at him. "Dora-Pandora . . ." he said to Dora. "Don't let the bedbugs bite."

"Cross your heart and hope you die, *Dickie*," she said. "See you, Colin."

They all left, but the girl.

"Is she your girlfriend?" Colin asked Dickie in a low voice.

"*Girl*friend? Where are you living, man?"

The girl was dancing, singing, "Come on, baby, light my fire . . . try to set the night on fire," moving languidly, sluggishly, to the beat, her arms waving off her shoulders like semaphores of lonely bliss.

"She lives upstairs," Dickie said. He flipped a quarter onto his palm and covered it with his other hand. "Heads I win," he said. Then, lifting his hand, "Aren't I a lucky bastard?"

The girl had large breasts, braless, flattened by her tight sweater, the nipples sticking up like mouths of sagging leather flasks. She had wide hips and a narrow waist, thin legs like sticks — graceless, yet, in their awkward frailty, more stirring than grace. Colin could not bear to look at her face.

"Let's get the show on the road," Dickie said.

She did not hear him. She continued to dance, legs together, arms outstretched, a yawn of a smile on her face like a sleepy child's. She could be teetering on a tightrope, unwary of toppling over.

"All yours," Dickie said to Colin, nodding toward the mattress. "The door locks itself."

He grabbed the girl by the arm and dragged her out of the apartment.

Colin picked up the tequila bottle from the floor where the girl had left it, and finished it off.

Half an hour later, he was still standing in the middle of the room. He stumbled. He righted his feet, having no idea where he meant to be going. He was alone in some strange apartment. He did not know how long he had been standing there. His mind was moving so slowly, anything his eyes looked at he perceived as if on a freeze-frame in a three-dimensional screen, unsteady and slightly out of focus. The sensation itself was not unpleasant, but what he saw scared him. The candlelight made the darkness over the opposite wall pulsate. Images, like holograms, wavered in midair: burned children, a woman with long black hair and outstretched arms kneeling on the ground, screaming.

The music had stopped long ago and he was hearing the silence only now, and there was no sound other than the sound of his heart, his blood throbbing in his veins to the slow funereal beat of a loud drum, *thump thump thump* — the vibration thudding through him, a tremor of pure fear, absolute, as if terror were the sole foundation of existence and the images pulsing off the wall were alive with desperation and death. Alive with death . . .

He turned on the overhead light, blew out the candles, and sat on the edge of the bed. His heart had suddenly calmed down, but his mind couldn't focus and thoughts glided off his consciousness as if no periphery surrounded his sense of self. It was the drugs and alcohol no doubt, yet something was happening inside him that had the stark force of sobriety, and despair cut in deeper, if with a blunter edge.

He didn't want to lie down. He was afraid to go to sleep. He sat crouching, his head hanging, his forearms resting on his thighs, his hands drooping over his knees. Thoughts began drifting through his mind — a row of ducks in a shooting gallery at a fair, single file, a steady, sluggish trail. They dropped down and, round and round, came up again — lapses and leaps of meaning.

dancing at the edge of the cliff . . . flowers in the hair . . . had he ever truly believed they could change the world . . . we think illusions buoy us . . . they're dead weight . . . suicide stones in the pocket . . . while we tread water . . . dancing at the edge of the cliff . . . dancing at the edge of a cliff . . . flowers in the hair . . .

◈

When he came home from Dickie's in the morning, Colin walked straight to the bathroom and splashed cold water on his face. He felt depleted; he hadn't had dinner, hadn't had breakfast—couldn't remember when he'd last eaten. Normally he could go without food the way a cactus can go without water. It was probably lack of sleep, but there was nothing to be done about that. He had never been able to sleep in daylight, even as a child, unless he'd been sick. He'd wait and see what food did for him, he thought. The guys from the band were coming over tonight, and he'd promised he'd have something new for them. He needed his energy back, and he needed it fast.

Taking his newly bought copy of Bruno Schulz's *The Street of Crocodiles* along, he went out to get something to eat.

During the week, at breakfast and lunchtime, the coffee shop down the street bustled with truckers and workers from nearby loft factories. At off hours and on Saturdays, it was filled with artists and bohemian riffraff. At the moment it was empty. The owner, George, sat by the register reading the *Daily News*, and Jorge, the short-order cook, stood with his back to the grill, staring ahead of him blankly. The only waitress covering the floor Saturdays was Lily, an older, booze-battered but still pretty woman. Looking like a pickled vestige of the fifties, with her roller-curled, teased hair, blue eye shadow, rouge, and matted red lipstick, she sat on the last stool at the far end of the counter, smoking and sipping black coffee, her starched pink uniform riding up her thighs.

It had taken her a while to warm up to the artists when they first started trickling in — one, two at a time like scouts for what would soon become an invading army. The grungy ragamuffin clothes had not fooled her one bit: college-educated rich kids — there was that too friendly, too bright look in their eyes. Most of them, she thought, were like lost children, who'd wandered away from home barefoot on a thorny road, believing it'd be a patch of clover.

She slid off the stool when Colin walked in and waited to see where he'd sit down. She liked him. He never had more than two words to say but was good people.

"Steak and eggs," he said before she approached him. "Black coffee."

"Did you hear that?" Lily shouted to Jorge.

Colin opened his book and bent his head over it.

Lily was not deterred.

"The girl from your building," she said, walking over. "I haven't seen her in a while. Her husband comes in every day. Are they still together?"

"They're still together," Colin said without raising his eyes.

Lily worried about Beatrice. The girl looked like her heart was breaking into pieces and she didn't yet know it. Nice, pretty girl like that and that husband of hers a prick like you've never seen. Go figure what made her stuck on him. Hadn't got her fireworks sparked — what gave a woman her pluck. Lily knew the look well — needing oil in the hinges.

She walked back to the counter and sat down.

"The cigarette machine doesn't give change," she said to George.

George did not lift his eyes from the paper.

"George, did you hear what I said?"

"I heard you."

Colin looked out the plate-glass window at the shining, frozen snow. There was a midday stillness to the light, no shadows, no wind. The steak sizzled on the grill, and the sputtering sound made the sudden silence all the more insistent and bleak.

He picked up *The Street of Crocodiles* and glanced dubiously at the back cover. The book was touted as an underground classic, with the sensibility of Proust and Kafka combined — something hard to imagine. Forget the hype. He had read randomly through it in the bookstore before deciding to buy it, and the writing was the kind he prized: tension between feeling and thought, a striving for clarity that made the beauty of the language seem incidental.

Bypassing the foreword, he started with the text:

> *In July my father went to take the waters and left me, with my mother and elder brother, a prey to the blinding white heat of the summer days. Dizzy with light, we dipped into that enormous book of holidays, its pages blazing with sunshine and scented with the sweet melting pulp of golden pears. . . .*

He didn't know what made him look up, nor was he startled to see Beatrice walking down the street. He stared at her, still immersed in the tranquil state he had sunk into while reading. She walked, glided, past the window and vanished. Shaken now, in delayed reaction, he bent his head over his book again, wondering where she might be going.

"Colin!" She was standing just inside the door. "You forgot your jacket last night."

She hesitated — fidgeting, looking away with anxious eyes — till he closed his book and pushed it aside.

"I just left it on your doorknob," she said, walking over. She sat down across from him in the booth. "I didn't knock. I thought you might be asleep."

"I don't sleep late. I'm not Ned," he said.

She stared him in the eyes as she unbuttoned her coat, then looked nervously away. "Lily," she called out. "Could I have a grilled cheese and bacon please?"

"Sure thing, hon," Lily said. "Want coffee?"

Without waiting for an answer, she brought over a cup. "Just made it." She put the cup down and patted Beatrice on the shoulder.

"Anything else, hon?" she asked.

Beatrice looked at her, confused. "The sandwich. Didn't I just order a sandwich?"

"You did . . ." Lily said, lingering. "Jorge has it on the grill already. Don't you, Jorge?"

She walked back to the counter.

"I'm famished," Beatrice said to Colin. "I want that sandwich so bad, I'm jumping out of my skin."

He pushed the bread basket toward her. "Have some bread."

"I don't want bread. I don't want anything else." Her eyes were wild, wide with hunger. She was breathing hard, fast. "I don't even like grilled cheese and bacon — I don't know what's happening to me. I threw up twice this morning."

"You're drinking too much."

"Isn't everyone . . ."

It wasn't the drinking, Beatrice thought. She had felt terrible earlier, but it wasn't like a hangover. Her head did not hurt, and after she threw up, the nausea did not recede. She had been seasick once, and it felt more like that: no steady foothold, blurry vision, dizziness like a vaporous vortex sluggishly pulverizing your insides.

The possibility she might be pregnant was too terrifying to face, like standing at the edge of a cliff and knowing the only way to keep your balance is not looking down.

She picked up *The Street of Crocodiles* and looked at the cover.

"Bruno Schulz! Bruno Schulz, Wallace Stevens, punk rock, the *AstroNuts* thing, abstract expressionist painting," she said. "I don't understand you, Colin."

"The music is a lark. I fell into it. I'm classically trained. *AstroNuts* I just put together. Painting is really my thing."

"Your thing . . ."

They were silent.

After some time, Lily brought over the sandwich. Turning her back to Colin, she bent close to Beatrice's ear and whispered, "It ain't worth it."

Beatrice started saying "what," but couldn't get the word out. Lily kept staring, now standing straight, her face daunting with disapproval and sour, like she was chewing on bitter cud brought up after a lifetime of swallowing. Yet her eyes had a bruised look of tenderness — kindness, perhaps.

"More coffee?"

Beatrice shook her head, and Lily went away.

"What was that all about?" Colin said.

"I don't know. Saturdays, it's Twilight Zone time in this place."

She blew furiously down at her plate. "Oh, God!" she said. "Do I have to wait for it to cool?"

She chomped off a large bite, grimaced in pain, and, barely chewing it, swallowed. Melted cheese and grease trickling down the corner of her mouth, she panted to get the heat out.

"I should have waited," she said, immediately taking another bite. She took two more and pushed the plate away. "That does it."

Colin had never seen her eat before, and the avid carnality bloating her face as she devoured her food shocked him. He didn't want to see it. Forcing himself to look at her, he pointed to his mouth and made a wiping motion.

She slid the back of her hand over her lips, stared at the bit of cheese stuck on her fingers, and licked it off.

"No one's here today," she said. "I've never seen it so empty."

They were silent again.

Beatrice thought of Ned lying in bed, his head propped up with pillows, chain-smoking. He'd heard her vomiting and had said nothing. Pain was so naked on her face it seemed to blur her features.

"Bea, are you okay?" Colin asked uncomfortably.

She picked up *The Street of Crocodiles* again and leafed through it.

"You change the name, you change the thing," she said, putting the book down. "It was first called *Cinnamon Shops.*"

"Bea, talk to me."

She lowered her eyes. "People read it differently, I bet,

when it was called *Cinnamon Shops*. Did you know he was a Jew? The Nazis killed him."

"Have it your way."

"My way . . . I *am* talking to you. You don't want to hear what I have to say. What d'you want me to talk about?"

"What you feel."

"What do *you* feel? What do you want from me?"

"I don't want anything from you."

"Well then."

She stared out the window, then back at him.

"People want to forget Christ was a Jew," she said. "The apostles were Jews. Paul was a Jew. Think of all the philosophers, the writers, the poets, the actors, the film directors, the musicians, the composers, conductors who are Jewish. Western culture rests on the shoulders of the Jews. Christian faith rests on the shoulders of the Jews."

Like every woman Colin had known, she argued over ideas as if she had an ax to grind. Like a marionette she looked to him, a marionette spitefully jerked by her strings, strident, peeved words clacking through her mouth.

"You're counting out the Greeks," he said.

"The Greeks . . . The Greeks are not about suffering and redemption. The Greeks are earthbound. They're about defying fate. They're about passion and pride. The Western world may have taken on their ideas, but it's alien to us, their pagan spirit. Anyway . . . we don't deny what we owe the Greeks. The Jews we persecute and despise. They gave and still give. We take it all — and have the Inquisition, pogroms, and the Holocaust to our credit."

"Who's 'we,' Bea?"

"I'm just saying . . . who christened *Cinnamon Shops, The Street of Crocodiles?*"

"Ah, we're still there," he said.

Beatrice wondered what he thought of Schulz. He read like reading was about the ability to discriminatingly admire and appreciate, and all he took from a good book was the validation of his mind, in which he took righteous pride. For her, a good book was a deeper, purer experiencing of life. A transformation in spirit and strength to the heart — that's what a good book was.

Schulz's work was bleak, she thought, yet feeling the despair that compelled the writing had been a comfort as she read him. In the face of such despair, the act of writing was protest, and protest was an act of faith. She'd felt this. Yet a numbing unease undercut the awe she had for his work. Her admiration for it, as the admiration she had for the work of other writers she thought great, cowed her regarding her own work, making her feel like a fraud.

Recently, she had started writing again. The new poems were confessional in tone, and her old lyrical impulse had turned to sentimentality and self-pity. She loathed her new voice and, even more, she loathed the content it spoke. What good was writing that served to validate one's puny personal life? Poor me — great me! A real writer's work, she thought — a work that lasted beyond its day — embraced, impersonally, all humanity. There was no I.

She wanted to be the real thing. She wanted to be the real thing, but how could she, when all she thought was I, I, I — who *am* I?

She had expressed some of these thoughts to Colin once,

not too long ago, and he had listened to her silently through-out, with what she had thought was condescending forbear-ance. All he had said was: "I didn't know you wrote." There hadn't been so much surprise in his voice as recoil from some unpleasant thought, as if she had confessed to a fact that had suddenly altered his opinion and compromised the feelings he had for her. Had she admitted to a character flaw, a tawdry past, or some hereditary degenerative illness, he wouldn't have looked more put out. Despite this, and though he did not ask, a day later she had shown him her newest poem. He'd read it standing, handed it right back to her, and said: "The language is beautiful." Just that.

She glanced at the book. "Do you like it?"

"It's a good book."

"It's the real thing," she said in an angry, contentious voice. "It's not a mere read—it's art. Art is the real thing or it isn't the real thing. There's no such thing as good art and bad art. There's art and would-be art. You can't pass a judgment of 'good' or 'bad' on the real thing. Truth isn't good or bad. It is what is."

Though the inability to let unreasoning beliefs go by was like a tic in his mind, Colin managed to restrain himself from responding. He said mildly, "I didn't know you had read him."

She looked at him with fury in her eyes. "You *assumed* I hadn't."

Colin pushed stiffly against the backrest of the booth. His hands lay flat, tense, on the table.

"I take it you want to leave," she said.

"When you're ready."

"I'm ready . . ."

She put three dollars down on the table.

"That should cover it," she said.

She stormed out.

Colin picked up both checks, paid, and followed her out. She was already halfway down the block. Instead of trying to catch up, he slowed his pace. He had no idea what had just happened.

◈

The hallway of the building was dark. There were maybe one, maybe two functioning lights per landing. The first four and top two stories were empty, decayed with years' abandon; the freight elevator had been disabled and its doors barred with crossing two-by-fours; the floor tiles and stairs were filthy. It was impossible to tell the color of the walls. In the dim light, the peeling paint looked vaguely gray, the grainy plaster underneath, a sharper hue like wet cement. There were cracks in the marble of the steps and the molding on the ceiling but otherwise the building was fortress-solid, having been constructed at a time when buildings were built with respect for human endeavor and with faith in the future. In its new incarnation, it evinced a more tenuous, if still idealistic, faith in life: "the future is now" was the held belief. Art made equal. Art made free.

When Ned and she first moved in, Beatrice had imagined she'd be at the forefront of a new frontier—helping remake the world, if indirectly.

Three years later, here she was — at the forefront indeed. *Ecce*, the artist's wife.

With a sense of total defeat, she dragged her feet up the steps. The landings on the uninhabited two top floors had no lights and, past the banister, the stairwell was an ascending vertical tunnel of deepening darkness. When she reached Colin's floor, she paused, looking up, to catch her breath, and her knees buckled.

Ned had taken pictures of her for his crow painting. He had gotten up early, at the same time she had.

"I want to take some pictures of you," he said. "I need them for my work."

He draped a white sheet over the table and asked her to lie naked on it. Reluctant, but too confused to resist, she obeyed. He positioned her right arm so that it hung over the edge, asked her to arch her head back and keep her lips open, then took several Polaroid pictures, having her lie still till each print had dried.

"One more," he said. "Bend your knees. Spread them." He aimed the lens between her legs. "That's it."

He walked to the studio, without a backward glance, and laid the photos on the drawing table in even rows of four.

"The lighting is not quite right," he said. "I didn't get what I wanted."

The shame she had had to overcome — a tingling quiver in the thighs, a shy tightness in her pelvis — erupted in shivers throughout her body. It was hard to stand up. Her legs were wobbly as when one first gets up after a long time lying sick.

He made her lie naked on a sheet-covered table like a corpse . . . he asked her to arch her neck, to smile . . . he asked her to open her legs, to spread her thighs . . . he held a camera to her cunt . . . he walked away without a word, without a glance back . . .

She moved away from the banister, closer to the wall, and sat down on a step.

Soon, she could hear Colin climbing the stairs. She was sitting just a few steps up from the landing. She walked back down and stood near his door. She did not look at him or speak as he approached.

Colin picked his jacket off the doorknob and hesitated putting the key in the lock. Clearly she was waiting to be invited in but still looked angry. It was like a dream come true — in all but the mood.

He looked at her. She did not meet his eyes.

"Would you like to come in?"

Beatrice didn't answer him. When he opened the door, she pushed in behind him and walked, past him, to the living area of the loft.

"Would you like some tea?" he said.

She threw her coat over the sofa and walked closer to him. At four steps away, she stopped, took off her sweater, and unbuttoned her blouse, baring her breasts.

"Don't do this, Bea."

"It's what you want."

"Not like this — not when you're feeling nothing."

"What d'you want me to feel? *Love?*" She lowered her eyes and looked at his crotch. "You think you love *me?*" she said. "You can't say it, can you?"

"You're not being your real self."

"My real self . . . And you know what that is."

He did not say anything.

"Right." She put her sweater back on and sat down on the sofa.

He remained standing, on the other side of the coffee table, a few feet away.

"I'll go make the tea," he said.

He set the kettle on the stove, placed two mugs on the counter, put tea bags in them, and waited for the water to boil.

"You're married," he said with his back to her.

"You're being honorable? Is that what you're telling me?" A sneering smile played on her lips. "You couldn't even say it, looking at me."

He came back, carrying a steaming mug in each hand.

"Is he upstairs?"

"He was when I left."

He sat down next to her.

She could feel him, could hear his shallow, faster breathing.

"Where should I put this?" she said, lifting the tea bag out of her cup.

He extended his arm, palm up.

"It's piping hot. It'll burn your skin."

"Ah, well. What's a little pain," he said.

She blew softly on her tea. Her hand holding the cup was trembling. Her lips started to tremble.

Colin watched and did not do a thing.

They were silent.

He sat hunched over, his elbows on his knees, his thighs spread wide, taking up most of the couch. Beatrice was wedged in at the other end. Civility, as the first refuge of injured pride, lay at the heart of her upbringing. Though in a mug, though from a tea bag, as soon as the tea was cool enough to sip, she drank it with ceremonious, stiff grace.

Colin owned the whole floor. The raw space directly below Perkins's place served as his painting studio. Adjacent to it, and enclosed by five-foot-high walls, was the *Astro-Nuts* office. The rest was a spread-out living area with a bed, an old Steinway grand, a large down-cushion sofa, and a round oak table surrounded by blond-wood, white-canvas chairs. Books were everywhere: on shelves, in stacks on the floor, piled every which way on the coffee table. Ring stains and cigarette burns mottled the layers of dust, music sheets and discarded junk mail lay scattered on the floor, rumpled clothes stuck out from open chest drawers, the bed was perpetually unmade. Yet, under the apparent disorder lay stultifying, latent order: he knew where everything was at any given moment.

"I haven't seen your place in daylight before," she said.

"It gets a lot of morning light from the back."

"We only get late afternoon light . . ."

Her voice trailed as she tried to find something else to say, to ease the tension. He wasn't helping, and her embarrassment and anxiety increased.

Her confidence in the power she thought she had over men had been the one last thing holding her together. Now it had lost purchase, and nothing was left at her core but want. She couldn't name what she was feeling: something like fear, like panic, like despair, like sexual hunger—all four combined.

She brought the mug to her lips but didn't take a sip. Her throat was tight and she was afraid she wouldn't be able to swallow. They hadn't, but the tension between them was as if they just *had* had sex. As after making it for the first time with a friend, there was—in both of them, she thought—that chilly awareness of the ungraspable strangeness of a person one thought one knew well.

She put the mug down on the coffee table and got up to leave.

Colin said nothing to stop her.

As she was walking out the door, he called out, "Your coat!"

"My coat... second time I seem to want to leave it behind."

She looked at him but he did not meet her eyes.

"See you later," he said.

◆

At her door, as she was putting the key in the lock, she suddenly sensed a presence behind her, not too close but close enough for her to feel she was being watched. She turned her head reflexively over her shoulder then jerked it back, too startled. Slowly, she turned around to look again: sitting on the floor, with his back leaning against the wall, was the boy she had seen near Dominic's the night of Faye's show.

He was wearing the same battered, black leather jacket, the same scuffed, square-toe black boots.

The image of him standing under the lamppost on the night they met had been floating through her mind for days, surfacing and fading amidst other thoughts; nonetheless, for the fleeting moment the memory lasted, her mind became still with wonder that he would have imprinted in her consciousness, a stranger met by chance. The more her life was getting out of control, the more she was starting to see in everything that was happening to her a hidden purpose or meaning.

Once might be chance, she thought. Twice showed the hand of fate.

Her heart was pounding. She didn't know what the fear was — not of the boy himself. She smiled at him, and he got to his feet, awkward and nervous, the way a shy young man stands for a woman.

"Could I have a glass of water?" he said.

She unlocked the door and walked in, leaving the door ajar. It was like she was in a trance: she heard his footsteps following her in; she went to the sink, picked up a glass from the draining rack, and filled it with water; as she was turning off the faucet, she noticed that the shelf where Ned kept his shaving brush, soap dish, and razor was empty; glancing to the side, she saw a note lying on the table — a large notebook page with two small lines written in pencil. She read it, as she walked by, without lifting it up.

Bea, I'm staying with Cyril for a while.
I'll call. WE NEED TO TALK — N.

"Here," she said.

The boy stood motionless, four feet away. Beneath the jacket, he was wearing a threadbare, loose-fitting blue sweater. His face was drawn, gleaming with sweat, his long hair stringy with grease. There was dirt under his fingernails.

"Here," she said again.

He took the glass from her hand and drank the water slowly in one draft.

"I know you from somewhere," he said.

"A few days ago, on Eighth Avenue —"

"I don't mean that," he said. "I thought I knew you from somewhere then."

His eyes were bleary, making it hard to see into him. It was more a feeling than clear perception: beautiful . . . a boy-delicate, man-stern sensibility . . . vulnerable . . . sullen . . . self-reliant . . . shy . . . willful . . . secretive . . . manipulative maybe. She was in a state of barely suppressed hysteria, and these impressions floated though her mind without cohering. Her heart continued to pound.

"What's your name?" she asked.

He opened his mouth, and silently closed it. "Chris," he said after a moment.

"You had to think about it?"

"It's Chris," he said. "What's yours?"

"Bea."

"Beatrice."

It startled her. Only her stepmother still called her that, and she did it in a distancing, prim voice.

He said again, softly, "Beatrice."

His face had lit up, the hollows under his cheekbones

filling out with light. He looked as ravishing again as the first time she'd seen him. Like an aura his beauty was, an afterimage of the image she had of him from then. He seemed intimately familiar suddenly — and more strange: beauty floated over his features, a transparent, impenetrable veil that hid nothing, revealed nothing, and shut him out from the world.

Who was he? Why did his beauty bring out such grief?

She wondered how long he'd been on the street. Couldn't be long. He was looking around him at the loft with discreet curiosity — the kind of manner that was usually bred though it could speak of innate delicacy of spirit. There was nothing coarse about him.

"How old are you?" she asked.

He lowered his eyes and said nothing. In a moment he looked in the direction of Ned's studio again, more openly this time.

"Are you an artist?" he said.

"No. No . . . I'm nothing."

"No one is nothing," he said.

She looked away.

He said again, under his breath, "No one is nothing."

He was still holding the empty glass, and she reached to take it from him. Their fingers touched. He looked at her, then away, too fast, but she'd seen the sex-dark spark in his eyes. The jolt was stronger than she'd ever felt. She'd never felt desire this sudden, this deep. She wanted him to take her — a boy, and she felt no-holds-barred submissive. He was strong — that's what it was. He was stronger than she. He knew more, had risked more. He stood vulnerable and alone in the world — like a stray — but he stood.

She couldn't look at him, couldn't speak—she was too uncomfortable being so near him. Why wasn't he reaching for her? Why wasn't he saying anything? He was scratching through the sweater at the underside of his elbow and forearm. His jeans were ripped below the right knee, his boots had muddy cracks in the leather, he was breathing hard . . .

Abruptly he turned his back to her and walked toward the door.

"Chris?"

"Thanks for the water," he said without turning around.

He hesitated before opening the door, then opened it slowly and closed it soundlessly behind him.

Beatrice went to the sink, filled the glass he had drunk from with water, and drank, putting her lips over the pale, milky stain his lips had left. It felt like a cold kiss. Liquor would make it feel right.

As she walked over to get the bottle, her eyes fell on Ned's note.

How large the page, how short the message.

She reached to open the cupboard and get the scotch but stopped with her fingers on the handle. Footsteps went slowly down the hall. Perkins's door creaked open, and closed. Moments later a harrowing scream pierced the wall, then soft, stifled moans and in counterpoint—slowly quickening—heartless sex grunts.

Till it was over, shudders heaved up from the base of her spine.

"No one," he'd said, "is nothing."

Cyril had been a star quarterback in high school. An athletic scholarship had allowed him to go to the University of Michigan, the only one in his graduating class to go on to college. The summer after freshman year, he worked at a gas station in Ann Arbor to save money. He did not go back to Scranton till the following Christmas. His old friends shunned him, even scorned him, as if college had put him one rung down, not up. Passing the football stadium his first day home, he felt like he was passing an open grave. How many had the crowd cheered to look at silently next year, when there was a new hero to hold up?

He had a dislocated right shoulder and a fractured forearm from training. Bruises covered him, pain he was supposed to bear without complaint. Though it was not something he could have articulated then, he understood how physical pain forges a deeper, emotional pain that isolates and hardens you. It was a cost of becoming a man. He had not thought it unjust.

In Vietnam, where "hard" had proven all too fragile and, under fire, terror made him quake inside, he asked: *Why?*

What for? Despise your feelings, despise your life — feel dead, before you're dead. He was a sensitive, reflective, reticent man. His parents were dour proud people — of Protestant English stock, in a town predominantly of Irish, Italians, and Poles. They felt it set them apart, and above. There was some of that in him too, and it made him seem overbearing, as did the blatant confidence with which he carried his muscular strength and height. But he was evenhanded, secretly sentimental, and overtly blunt — to the bone, dignified and decent.

The worst scar of the war had been seeing his moral foundation erode. Before long, fear had denuded his will to a savage, merciless instinct to survive. Hatred and a vicious impulse to vengeance had stunned any vestigial sense of his old self, the voice that whispered, "This isn't you." It *was* him. He felt what he felt, he did what he did. *The truth shall set you free.* He had repeated this to himself without irony, and the bitterness had been almost sweet.

While he was growing up, the industry that had given the town and the surrounding area vigor was already long into decline. Where farmland and forests used to stand, the landscape was now scourged with acid deposits and black soot. His first view from the window of the bus, coming home after his tour, was a flatland of short shrubbery and shale outcroppings he'd seen numberless times before, without having the ugliness seep in.

So much looked gray and skeletal: the rail tracks and high trestles, the wrought-iron bridges . . . The sprawl of the city from the riverbank inland was haphazardly gridlike, with warehouses in empty, cracked-asphalt lots, low, decrepit white stucco houses, and a scattering of rust-red brick buildings—beautiful and dreary, like scant blooms on a blighted tree. Small things, later—the edges of linoleum curling off the baseboards in his parents' kitchen, the paint peeling on his father's old Chevy, the faint smell of sewage and mold in the house—made him close his eyes.

His father, too, had been to the war—that other, "heroic" war. His silver star and two purple hearts lay hidden in a drawer. He never talked about them. A hero hangs his hat by the door when he enters his home. A silent, brooding, hard-working, hard-drinking man was how Cyril always remembered him. He had no memory of him before he was four. Ned, born right after the war, was the child of his parents' new life together; Cyril had been pushed aside. Obedient, dutiful, all he'd ever heard from his father was, "You do me proud, son."

It had been the first thing he'd said to him when Cyril came back, while he was still standing on the doorstep.

There had been nothing Cyril could say in return.

For five days, he did not leave the house. He slept, watched TV, had dinner with his parents, got drunk alone on the porch, went to bed leaving the door to his room open, the hallway light on.

At the end of the week, on a Sunday, he borrowed his father's car and drove to Wilkes-Barre to visit Matt Coles, an army buddy who had finished his tour a month before him. He had not called first. The house was about a dozen miles past the edge of town, on a lot abutting a small copse of pine and, in back, empty fields stretching down to the river. A small tan truck was parked in the driveway, its tailgate hanging open. He walked past it, and was moving toward the front door when he heard a rhythmic creaking noise coming from the backyard — something like a door swaying on a rusty hinge but with a fuller, blunter sound.

The house was silent and seemed empty. He walked around to the yard and saw Coles sitting in a tire swing roped to a branch of an oak tree. He was paddling his feet in a slow toe-to-heel motion, head bent, hands on his lap steadying an Early Times pint. He raised and turned his head, showing no surprise.

"I heard the car and thought you were my sister, man," he said.

The yard was overgrown with weeds, yellow dandelion flowers sparkling amidst purple clusters of hyssop and dense grass. An old Frigidaire, same model as the one Cyril's parents still had in their kitchen, was standing by the tool-shed. Other pieces of junk, choked by the weeds, flashed gleams of rusty metal and a variegated sheen of colored plastic.

Cyril sat down on a barrel lying on its side five feet off the swing.

"How long you been back?" Coles said.

"Don't know — ten days . . ."

They were silent.

"Heard from Luke," Coles said. "He wrote me a letter."

"What did he say?"

"Don't know, man. He wants to start a chinchilla farm. Talked about chinchillas in the whole damn letter. You got to electrocute them, to get the fur. Strap them in little electric chairs, fry the fuckers."

Cyril put a cigarette in his mouth.

"How are you holding up?"

"Don't know, man," Coles said. "Sometimes I wish I was back there. I get these nightmares — they don't let up. Can't tell day from night. It's like flashbacks from acid. Better live it than dream it."

"I haven't had one single dream since I came back," Cyril told him. "I sleep so deep, I wake up and I don't know where I am, like my room at home is a time capsule and there's no outside back of the walls."

"We're all time capsules, man — walking about . . . Life's rolled on by — can't catch up to it. Lesson one."

"What's lesson two?"

"There ain't no lesson two — that's lesson two."

Cyril looked at the rolling fields and past them, the steady rippling flow of the river.

"It's beautiful here."

"Paradise on earth," Coles said, taking a long pull of bourbon and passing the bottle to Cyril. "Paradise on earth. Six feet under, and I'd really be in heaven."

He laughed.

It was the raucous, manic laughter they had all laughed with over there. The common wisdom was: you cry your heart out once, then you laugh. Cyril had not had his one cry, but he'd had his laughs, and then some. He had not laughed as hard, as much his whole life. Anything touched him, he was an exploding land mine of jokes and jibes. But it had all gone out of him suddenly.

"I think I may mow all this down and plant some weed," Coles said.

He looked like he had slept in his clothes and had not washed for days. The breeze was now blowing from his way, and the stench overwhelmed the flower scent in the air. Cyril tried to squelch the sense memory: the cesspool smell in his mouth and in breaths close to his face, the stink of dysentery shit and sun-drying piss, of jungle rot and suppurating feet, of death that, like musk, left an oily residue in the nostrils. Hours later, far away, one could still smell it.

Yes, he did cry once. He was fucking a bar girl on a straw mattress on the floor, when the smell from the decaying, blown-to-bits child he'd slipped over twelve hours before swept up his nose like a spurt of soft air. He had been but seconds in her. As he pulled out, she stayed still, her hands clenched into tiny fists, her face flaccid. Like most of them, she was thin and small, her breasts elliptical puffy folds of skin, the nipples so dark they gleamed in the muted light like tar and were swollen, smooth, inordinately large, and dented in the center like a child's. He hadn't had wide sexual experience with women, and at first glance they had stirred in him a hankering as for something luring and deeply forbidden. "Ceereel," she said. "No money back. Free next time." As he was zipping his pants, a sob caught in his throat and his eyes flooded.

"Seriously," Cyril said, "what are you doing for the rest of your life?"

"You asking me on a date, man?" Coles grinned and reached out to take the bottle back from Cyril's hands. "I *am* serious. What d'you plan on doing?"

"I'm going to New York," Cyril said, resolve coming over him just that moment. "My kid brother lives there."

When he mustered out, between last month's and previously unpaid leave pay, he had five hundred dollars. With that, and no plans concerning what he would do when he got there, he arrived in New York City on a Greyhound bus. Port Authority had the drab, oppressive, dreary aura of other bus depots he'd been through, but seemed less desolate, for the buzz of the milling crowds. The garbage-spattered floors, the paint on the walls, the fixtures, everyone's face and clothes looked used up — bleak, in the way cheap things and the destitute age — yet it all gave off an energy that swept him off his feet. It was late evening. Outside, a soft gray light spread like shadow, muting the grunge and dirt on Eighth Avenue as far as his eyes could see. He felt a force of life surround him, distant and close, like the waning flow of the sea near a shore.

The city was going bankrupt, crime and poverty were rampant, but the dark, seething vitality running through it was about to turn things around. He had no way of knowing that. In his view then, he was placing a bet against the house, gambling to beat the odds. It took him little time, however, to see it would be a sure gain. Real estate. It had already started in SoHo. Staying with Ned and Beatrice in their loft the first month, he was convinced it was bound to spread farther downtown.

Ned and all Ned's friends, by hook and crook, had gotten 4-Fs. Even knowing what he now knew of patriotism and the war, Cyril felt contempt for them, but also an odd compassion. Cowardice, unless disproved, cannot be lived down. At what price the high moral ground? Pacifism, feminism, civil rights, gay rights, human rights . . . they all thought they were changing the world, being nice.

To tell the future, follow the money.

It wasn't plain cynicism. There was a lot of rage in him.

After staying afloat on construction work for a while, he did a couple of drug runs—a truckload of marijuana from Miami, cocaine from Chicago. He had the connections to go big-time, but did not want to pay the Devil more than his due. He used the drug money to buy an old Federal-style town house on Greenwich Street, and continued to deal small amounts, whatever came his way. To gut the building, he had hired a crew; the renovation he was now working on slowly by himself. The plan was to convert each floor into small lofts. He had not decided yet if he would rent or sell, but either way he figured he'd have the down payment for a larger building he had his eye on down the block.

He was now living on the ground floor of the house he owned. There was no heat or hot water yet. Clear insulating plastic covered the windows, and a large electric heater was set in the middle of the room. His bed was a double mattress on the floor. A nine-inch black-and-white TV was propped on a chair across from it, and two more chairs sat on opposite sides of a table at the far end of the room.

This moment he was standing by the stove waiting for water in the saucepan to boil. Ned was sitting at the table.

"What's a while?"

"A while . . ." Ned said. "I was thinking I could move my studio upstairs till you sell the place—sleep there and come down to use the bathroom."

"She threw you out?"

"I left her."

"What are you going to do for money?"

"I thought you'd lend me some till I get a job. Or I could work it off—help you with the work here. I could start Tuesday. Monday I'm moving my stuff out. I have a friend who has a truck. I won't need you for that."

"Looks like you have it all figured out."

"It's been coming a long time," Ned said.

Cyril spooned instant coffee into the cups and stirred in the water. He slid one toward Ned, picked up the other one and had a sip.

"How did she take it?"

"I don't know. I left her a note. There's no talking to her. I tried to last night."

"What did she say?"

"She said nothing. She cried, then fell asleep."

Cyril looked away.

"You don't know what she's like. Can't tell you the times I've tried to leave her. You don't know what love is till you slam the door, then stop halfway down the stairs and can't go on."

Cyril kept his eyes down. *You don't know what love is till you've waited in darkness before a closed door,* he thought. The hope that Beatrice would have him brought back the loneliness and despair he thought he'd beat out of himself in Nam. Burned out, and still hurting . . .

Ned opened his cigarette pack, saw it was empty, tossed it aside, and took a cigarette from Cyril's pack. "Filtered! Since when?" He lit one and blew out the match with a loud short breath like a scornful humph.

"I'm done with her," he said.

Cyril looked at him. He hadn't had much affection for him when they were kids, but did have respect. Ned had been scrawny and got beat up a lot yet never told who beat him or tried to hide his bruises. He'd had some backbone of dignity then. Now, just looking at him, Cyril felt plain shamed to be blood.

"You're an asshole," he said.

Ned looked him in the eye. "I know you've been wanting to make it with her. You think I'm blind?" he said evenly.

The phone rang.

Neither one looking at the other, they let it ring. It rang a long time, stopped, and immediately rang again a yet longer time.

◆

On the following Wednesday, March 5, Carol Dyer was scheduled to have gum surgery. Dyer already had a pin in her hip and had had her right knee operated on twice. The dentist had put the fear of God in her, telling her she might be losing her teeth. There was a lot to feel sorry for herself about, yet she had decided to drop by the office before her appointment and make sure Beatrice would be all right left alone.

The last two days, Beatrice had come to work in clothes that looked like they had been slept in. Her skin had been pale and pasty, her eyes glassy, and her hair clumpy with grease. She had done no work other than answer the phone and that, in a sluggish, bleak voice. Dyer didn't know if it was drugs or some kind of breakdown. When she had asked her what was wrong, Beatrice had said it was weather allergies and, really, she was fine.

Today, the glow was back on her skin. She looked healthy and in good spirits. Youth, Dyer thought. One day the face of death and the next fresh as a daisy.

"I see you've washed your hair."

"My hair . . . yes," Beatrice said. "I thought you weren't coming in today."

"I have a thing or two to do."

Dyer went into her office, rummaged through the papers on her desk, pretending to look for something, and came back out. A gnawing worry remained.

"Look here, Bea. I suppose you don't want to talk about what's wrong, but know I'm willing to listen."

Beatrice avoided her eyes.

Dyer hesitated. "The manuscript I gave you Monday?" she said. "See if you can read through it today."

After Dyer left, Beatrice tried to catch up with her tasks. It was three o'clock by the time she got to the manuscript. The title page read *The Rhymes and Times of Grand Band* by Adam MacAdam. There was a note taped under the title:

Carol,

This is god-awful, I know — but he's my accountant's son. (He had polio as a child, which left him paralyzed, and now he has lupus.)

ELEANOR ROSSI

Eleanor Rossi was another one of Dyer's best-selling authors. She had used a ballpoint pen, and when Beatrice peeled off the note, she saw that the words had been embossed on the page and could be easily read. She tried to rub the grooves smooth, but to no effect. Thinking that wetting the paper might help, she spit on the page and rubbed again. It worked but left a large crinkly stain, more flagrant than the imprint of the note had been. What would the poor author think? She put her finger in her coffee, wiped it on the bottom of the cup, and set the cup down over the stain twice, stamping intersecting coffee rings. That should throw him off the scent, were he to suspect the stain was spit.

She was hyperventilating and sweating as she turned to the first page. The typed characters swam in front of her eyes, gray marks like specks of flurrying ash. She had to blink several times before she could focus, and then she thought her mind was playing tricks on her:

> Monica played the harmonica. Sanjo played the banjo. Mariano played the piano. Marcello played the cello. Tina played the concertina, Verna-Lyn the violin and Pauline the tambourine. Viola would naturally have played the viola but she had no arms. This was a severe concern to all, except for Lola who now could claim her place with grace. It was decided that Viola should change her name to Nance and pair off with Vance. He would teach her to tap dance. The two, already chums, would be substitutes for drums. That left Morgan who had no money to buy, or rent, an organ. To his great chagrin, the band refused to chip in. He could call himself Russ and make a fuss but being a good chap, he put on his cap and left for Bolivar,

the bar, to meet his friend Louie who only drank
Drambouie —

The production manager, Lois, walked in.

"Get Carol to look at this, first thing in the morning," she
said, dropping a new mockup jacket for *Byron: Hot Youth* on
Beatrice's desk. "See if you can make her see the light. The
type is too dark and heavy — too doom and gloom for 'hot
youth.' "

"Lois, would you read the first few sentences of this?"

Lois walked around the desk and bent over Beatrice's
shoulder.

"It's a hoot," she said. "I guess."

On her way out, Lois stopped at the door, turned around,
and stood leaning against the jamb with her right arm raised
and her left hip thrust out.

"So, Bea. I'm going to wear a red wedding dress and a
black veil."

Lois was soon to be married to a fireman, in what would be
her third wedding. She was thirty-nine and he was ten years
younger.

"In church?"

"Kidding. Gotcha!"

Beatrice tried to smile.

"Lois, could I ask you something? Were you in love with
your first husband?"

"Thought I was."

"You didn't know?"

"Thought I knew. You don't really know till the next man
comes along and makes you feel less passionate, or more."

She was a big woman, bottle blond, and had a broad face

with shrewd, vivacious dark eyes. Soft laugh dimples around her mouth gave her a look of youthfulness and sweetness, all the more winsome, riding on a brassy manner.

"Why?"

"Just asking . . ."

Lois stared at her.

"Whatever it is, you're pretty as a picture and sexy as all get-out. You have nothing to worry about. You need to talk, give me a holler. Have to run back to my office."

Beatrice felt utterly exhausted, and there were two more hours of work, then the book party for Jane Worth's new novel, *Rachel's Lot*. She couldn't stand Jane Worth. She'd met her at the publication party for her previous book and had thought her singularly obnoxious — so humorless, self-absorbed, supercilious, and prim, she could have been a sour suburban housewife protesting too hard her social ranking. As for her prose, it was somberly plain and sturdy — something like sackcloth, but with a tighter weave. Her novels had a dour realism that Beatrice would respect if the effect were not merely dreary. In the gap between "good" and "god-awful," she thought, if *Rhymes and Times* was the steamy froth, *Rachel's Lot* was the boiling muck below.

What was she doing reading this thing?

What was she doing here?

The trust fund her grandmother had set up for her after her mother's death gave her enough to live on, if not lavishly. She hadn't needed the job. She had taken it, wanting to feel she was someone, not just someone's wife. It had been, too, the need to assuage her guilt over having money, as Ned never let her forget how hard he'd had it growing up and how, by contrast, she'd been coddled against the harsh realities of life and made to think she had a right to skim the fat while others were starving. Not that he had any compunction over taking her money — acting, to boot, like he was suffering her to be good to him. It wasn't enough that she supported him. He expected her to clean after him and cook for him. If she ever served leftovers, he pushed his plate away, saying she should feed such scraps to a dog. After she started working — a week into the job — he started berating her, attaching to her the contempt he had for the bourgeoisie's sensibility and values — from their lily-livered need for propriety, to their fake respectability, hypocrisy, and sexual repression, to their deliberate or inadvertent exploitation of the masses; and, last but not least, as it was the one accusation that proved her demonstrably in the wrong, their conformity to dress code. She was finally showing her true colors, from flower-child garb to career-wear: back to the Bendels clothes and Sesci boots her Granny bought for her.

She hadn't had the honesty, the self-respect, the *dignity* to tell Ned to fuck off.

Slumping lower in her chair, she stared at the Byron book jacket. It was a photograph of an 1812 engraving from a portrait of the poet by George Sanders. The face was soft and plump, gentle and sensitive around the mouth. It could be a woman's but for the blunt, straight-staring look in the eyes — those of a man who believes he can take from the world what he needs by right.

She walks in beauty, like the night . . .

Who had the woman been? Had Byron passed on her love, to praise her in verse? He was dust, she was dust — the words remained.

The smiles that win, the tints that glow,
But tell of days in goodness spent, —
A mind at peace with all below,
A heart whose love is innocent.

She had memorized it in seventh grade. She'd had to memorize one poem a week all through junior high. A few months into it, she had tried to write a poem herself, but couldn't get the form right. The words had gushed out with spontaneous rhythm, forming no rhyme or prosodic break at the end of the line — an endlessly unfurling streamer of images and diffuse, if sincere, emotion. It did not look, did not *feel*, like a poem. When she told her English teacher, a Mr. Farnsworth, who'd praised her papers in an effusive, fawning manner, he did not ask to see it. "You," he said, "the way you look! You should be having — will have — poems written about you. Why want to write?"

Tears had come to her eyes then. Now they were there again, suddenly there, before she could feel them well up, springing from sadness so deep, a place so hidden, it was as if her body were crying all on its own. They fell, and kept falling, down her face, and it was as if she had known no other feeling than this unbearable grief, would never know any other feeling.

Afraid someone else might walk in, she went to the bathroom to wash her face and try to get the red out of her eyes. Her lids were swollen and the underlying hollows bloated, but there was a soft, serene-seeming, beautiful glow on her face.

Simone Weil had written that a beautiful woman looking

in the mirror may think that's all she is; an ugly woman looking in the mirror *knows* that's not all she is. Beatrice tried to
stare harder at her reflection, but it made her too anxious and
she looked away. Nothing connected. Why had she been born
with that face? Why was anyone born with a particular face
when it did not match what one was, what one felt, inside? It
was like being born with a mask — randomly beautiful or ugly.

An ugly woman, she imagined, knew she was loved for herself when she was loved. Beauty . . . beauty got you laid easy
enough, that was for certain. Beauty got you fucked.

She waited for the puffiness around her eyes to go down
and went in to see the editor in chief, Jackson Marks, and tell
him she was not feeling well and would not be going to the
party.

"You'll rally," he said. "All you have to do is stand around
and smile. Let me give you some friendly advice. You won't
get anywhere in this business — any business — unless you
play your cards right." He had just come back from his usual
three-martini lunch, and his eyes gleamed. He loosened his
tie and adjusted his belt a hole to the left. "I have my eye on
you."

He did have his eye on her all right. He had made several
oblique passes that always ended with his saying, "A girl like
you could go far."

She went home to dress up. The party was at a new, trendy
gallery in SoHo not far from where she lived. She decided to
go on the early side, make her appearance, and leave. She
could walk there and back — it wouldn't have to be a big deal.

She arrived at six thirty sharp, when the party was supposed to start. As she was about to go through the door, she

saw Jane Worth coming up close behind. She stepped aside to let her pass, and wished her good luck with her book.

"Thank you, I'm sure," Worth said, her face stern and tight.

The gallery was already packed. The paintings on the walls made the gathering seem like an art opening, though, being that publishing had not quite shed its tweed-jacket image, there was no mistaking the book crowd for an art crowd. Still, the same preening drunken excitement, the same name-dropping, adulating din filled the room.

She was the youngest person there, a merely decorative presence — the single reason Jackson Marks had insisted she come. He was ogling her, then averting his eyes, while his attention was focused on the conversation he was having — obviously what truly mattered. She tried to move about so as to keep her back to him and stay clear of Jane Worth, who was holding court in the center of the room.

The bar, a long foldaway table covered in white cloth, was set up near the far wall. The barman was around her age, an actor the company had frequently used before, and Beatrice had spoken with him at some length at the last Christmas party. He was handsome in a bland, blue-eyed, blond-hair way — the kind of face that stands out but later one can't recall distinctly — and had a debonair, polite manner, too gracious to be unaffected.

Beatrice remembered him and their conversation in sharp detail. He was from the South and had dropped out of Duke to take up acting. His name was Nick Bradley, but his friends called him Ace. He had a calico cat that fetched like a dog. He'd been in a dandruff shampoo commercial and had modeled men's clothes for photo ads. Staring at her wedding ring, he had said: "The best ones are taken."

Now, when her turn came to be served, he made eyes and said, "Bernice, is it?"

"Beatrice."

"Right! What would you like?"

"A scotch."

He poured her a Johnnie Walker Black.

"Only the best for the best," he said, letting his fingers touch hers as he handed her the glass.

She walked away slowly, trying to have a sip of the scotch, but her throat constricted and she couldn't swallow. A voice whispered in her mind: *What am I doing here, what am I doing here, what am I doing* here? Here — the sense of "here" expanding over the outside world, the universe — life.

She wanted to run out but her body dragged as if it were weighted down.

"Ah, Bea," Lois said, sidling up to her. "I've been looking for you. Some of us gals are going out to dinner later. You want to come?"

"I can't."

"Oh, come on! Tell that husband of yours you're gonna have some girl fun. It'll fix him right."

"I can't," Beatrice said again, trying to force some vivacity in her voice and blushing for the lie. "I can't! I have other plans."

"Other plans . . ." Lois said, lifting her drink to her lips and giving a thumbs-up with her free hand. "Quite the little social bee, aren't you?"

Beatrice picked up her coat from the back room and made her way out, pushing through the crowd.

It was freezing outside. Her teeth started chattering — from the cold, from anxiety, she didn't know. Her whole body started shaking. She hurried to put on her coat. As she was buttoning up, her forearms grazed over her breasts. She had to take a deep, long breath. No harder loneliness than the gentle ache in them . . .

All right now, she thought. *Keep breathing,* she thought. *All you have to do is concentrate on breathing,* she thought. *All you have to do is stop thinking,* she thought.

◈

Faye sighed, to get some air into her lungs. Not to mention her goodwill, her mind was beginning to wear out. Bea had come over without phoning, had asked her to cancel her dinner plans, had enthroned herself in the large wing chair like it was her house and Faye, sitting uptight at the edge of the couch, the poor relation, dressed in her Sunday best to impress. She needed to talk, she said. Well, she had been talking nonstop for hours, her voice high-pitched and hoarse, her face frozen, like a two-bit actor with stage fright. Vintage Beatrice — how she got when she couldn't tell her ass from her brain: "When self- and outer-defined identity are not the same, reality has no hold" . . . "beauty is a veil of happiness that only love can lift" . . . "stellar conjunctions determine coincidence" . . . " 'star-crossed lovers' is no figure of speech" . . . "there is nothing random" . . . "grace is the acceptance of necessity with free will" . . .

Cymbals and drums heralding the pièce de résistance: Morose Limpcock, a.k.a. Colin Ambrosius Southgate, was her would-be white knight, some pretty young boy she'd met on the street, Master Right—but for the fact he might be queer—and by the way, Ned had left her. Now, she was reminiscing about Halloween, age seven.

"Remember when we got dressed as marigolds?"

"It was daisies, I think."

"It was marigolds," Beatrice insisted. "Remember the caps we had to wear?"

"No, I don't."

"They were cloche hats and had a stubby stem-thing sticking out on top."

"Where is this going?"

"They were made of satin. Mine kept falling off. Yours stayed on."

"And the point is?"

"The point is . . . you've always kept it together. You look all over the place, but you always have it together."

"I'm sure it was bobby pins," Faye said. "The cap—it was fastened to my hair."

"Simple as that," Beatrice said, her eyes blank with silent thought. "I guess . . . I guess, if the shoe fits wear it; if it doesn't fit don't wear it."

Her voice had a comic gravity as a small child's saying, newly discovered, something trite, and Faye snorted an unstoppable laugh. Beatrice blushed. Upstaging silent dignity would come next, Faye thought—then, one of two lines: *Sorry I said a word,* or *I'm a fool to be friends with you.*

It didn't happen.

"I want to go barefoot," she went on, earnestly as before. "I want to live my life. I want to find the real me."

"Turn the page, Bea! Turn the page! You *are* the real you. All you have to do is turn the page. Admit you made a mistake to marry Ned and turn the page."

If Bea heard her at all, it didn't penetrate.

"With Chris, who I just told you about, there was a moment there that I felt real again, as I had in the beginning with Ned. He called me Beatrice, *Beatrice,* and it was like I'd been dead and suddenly felt my heart beating again. He said my name and his voice sounded—"

"Apparently, like the trumpet call sounding the Second Coming."

"You understand *nothing.*"

Her eyes were vile with hatred and, still, evoked desire.

"You're getting over the edge, Bea," Faye said, looking away. "You've got to get a grip."

Beatrice did not respond.

In a moment, she stood up and said in a chilly, huffy voice, "Do you have a wrapper?"

"A wrapper?"

"A robe, you know . . . My clothes are too tight. I'm bloated."

She put her foot on the seat of the armchair, lifted her skirt, and started to unhook her stockings from her garter belt, then stopped and turned her head over her shoulder.

"Well? Will you stay sitting there?"

Faye went to the bedroom and brought out a plaid night-shirt.

"That's all I have that's clean."

Beatrice had taken off her clothes, and all she had on was a black nylon slip with opaque lace down to the waist. She grabbed the nightshirt from Faye's hands and put it on over her slip.

"Who got you this?"

"I bought it."

"It's so not you."

"I like to surprise," Faye said.

Beatrice picked up her clothes and folded them neatly over the back of the chair, the garter belt and her stockings side by side on top.

"Why aren't you wearing pantyhose?"

"Ned likes me in stockings."

"Does he . . ."

Faye thought of Ned and having him in her mouth — her secret love and betrayal of Bea, the denied desire — his cock a link to her, for a moment sweet.

"He's not going to come back to you," she said quietly. "You've got to get him out of your mind."

They were standing three feet apart. Beatrice took a step back.

"You're free, Bea. You can have your life back. Nothing is stopping you. You can have anything you want. All you have to do is turn the page and pull yourself together."

"I've got nothing left. There's nothing holding me together."

"You've got everything. Listen to me: you're beautiful, you're young, you're rich. People would kill to be that."

"*That*," Beatrice said. "No one is a *that*. I'm not a *that*."

She sat down again.

Faye remained standing. She was in spike heels and a black silk, ankle-length fitted dress with a mandarin collar and side slits up to the knee.

"I should go change," she said.

She turned to go to the bedroom.

"Can you do me a favor tomorrow morning?" Beatrice said. "I want you to call my boss at ten fifteen. I'll give you the number."

Faye turned around. "Why ten fifteen?"

"She'll be answering the phone by then — she'll have figured out I'm not coming in. Otherwise, she'll let it ring. Tell her I'm sick. Tell her I have mono and I'll be out indefinitely."

"What would that be, mouth mono? You couldn't be calling her yourself?"

"I have mono and it made me weak and I fell down and broke my jaw," Beatrice said, breathing fast. "I want to quit."

"That's crazy, Bea. Call her and tell her you want to quit."

Beatrice looked away.

"I can't. I can't face her. You've got to help me," she said. "You've got to help me! You've got to help me!"

"I'll see what I can say," Faye said. "It will be all right. Everything will be all right . . . Want to spend the night?"

Beatrice shook her head no.

"You shouldn't be alone."

"I *am* alone."

Faye walked up to her and knelt by the chair. She put her hands on Beatrice's thighs and stroked her, splaying her fingers to a kneading grip.

"You're not alone," she said.

Beatrice pushed her away and got up. She had started to cry, and Faye tried to put her arms around her.

"I'm too upset for this," Beatrice screamed. "Once and for all, Faye. Stop it!"

"Why don't you go to hell," Faye said.

Beatrice picked up her clothes off the chair and started to dress with slow movements as if her body were stiff and ached. When she was done, she walked past Faye without looking at her and opened the hallway closet to get her coat. Keeping her back to her, she said evenly:

"So long, Faye."

After leaving Faye's apartment, Beatrice went home and straight to bed. The next morning she woke up at eight by force of habit, but as she was filling the kettle with water, she suddenly felt so drowsy, her mind blacked out as if she were about to faint. She went back to bed and slept till noon. She got up and walked to the sink to refill the kettle with fresh water, but reached for the scotch bottle instead and poured herself a drink.

To avoid the light coming from Perkins's side late at night, she had dragged the bed farther down the wall, into Ned's studio space that now stood empty. There was the bed and, in the far corner, the racks storing his old work. They covered an eight-by-twelve-by-ten-foot area and were draped with sheets, looking like a freight crate abandoned on a dock. He'd left everything he no longer had a use for behind. Including her — hello and good-bye.

She sipped her drink, poured herself two more, then started drinking out of the bottle till she felt woozy enough to crawl back into bed.

It was four o'clock. She slept without waking till five the

next morning. As soon as she opened her eyes, her mind was alert and clear, her body as if weightless — no tightness anywhere, no hangover. She felt eerily peaceful. After eating a huge breakfast — a cheese omelet, home fries, sausage, and four pieces of toast — she set to cleaning the loft. She vacuumed, mopped, dusted; she scrubbed the shower stall, the stove, the oven inside and out. When she was done, she took the clothes Ned had left behind and folded them neatly into a small suitcase.

Swelling waves, now of anxiety, now of rage, began washing through her. Taking deep breaths to steady herself, she walked to the wall phone in the studio and dialed Cyril's number.

It was around ten by then.

"It's me," she said. "I want you to go wake up your . . . *brother* and get him down to the phone. I'll wait."

"How are you, Bea?"

"Go do it."

"He's not upstairs. He hasn't been sleeping here nights."

"Go get him!" she screamed. "Go get him, wherever he is."

"I don't know where he is."

"I want his things out of here. I want him to take the storage space down! I want everything out! Out!"

"I'll tell him."

"Now! Today!"

"I'll ask him to call you when I see him."

"I don't want to talk to him. I *don't . . . want . . . to talk* to him."

"Calm down."

"I don't want to calm down!"

"He's tried to call you."

"When! On his way to spending the night wherever he's spending the night? Just back from her?"

She slammed down the receiver. Immediately she dialed back and screamed with stuttering, sobbing rage: "I'll rip . . . rip his pain . . . paintings to shreds. I'll throw them out the win . . . window."

"You're not being yourself, Bea."

"I am — am being myself. You don't — don't — know me."

"I know you, Bea. You need to calm down. You don't mean what you're saying. You're too upset."

"Too upset. Ah! That's all it is. I'm too upset. I feel better already."

She slammed down the receiver again.

He called right back.

"If it will make you feel better," he said, "I'll come take his things."

"I want the paintings out. I want the storage space taken down."

"I can do that."

"Now! I want it done now."

"I have a meeting at the bank at two. How about four this afternoon?"

"All right." She stayed silent a moment, then said in a calmer, soft voice, "I'll make us dinner."

"I'd like to take you out."

Her voice pitched up. "You don't want me to cook. You're afraid it's going to be like on your birthday."

"It isn't that."

"Yes, it is! You're afraid I'll mess up. You think I'm a bad cook."

"I just thought it'd be good for us to go out. I want to treat you to something nice."

"I can make something nice here. It will be good."

"I'm sure it will be."

"I'll see you at four then."

"Could be earlier," he said. "I don't know how long the meeting will run. I said four to be on the safe side."

"I want to know precisely when you're coming. Let's make it four exactly."

He sighed audibly. "On the dot," he said.

◆

She took a shower and washed her hair. She thought she'd wear jeans and her white angora cardigan, but when she put them on, the jeans were too tight to zip up without lying on her back and raising her legs up, and her breasts pulled so hard on the sweater, the buttoned placket stretched into gaping vents. She tried a skirt. She tried her pleated pants, several dresses — nothing felt comfortable around her midriff. The only outfit that gave her some berth was a low-cut, princess-style purple velvet gown she'd last worn two years ago at a New Year's Eve party. She'd have to wear high heels and sheer stockings with it, and if she went that far, why not all the way? Heavy eye makeup, her waist-long, single-strand pearl necklace, painted nails.

Now, to the question of the food, she thought. The meal! She wanted dinner to go smoothly, without having to get up to serve this and that or fuss, keeping a zillion side dishes warm. Something that could go into one pot. Soup — a hearty soup. Mrs. Engle, the housekeeper back home, made a beef and vegetable soup that "could raise the dead," as she put it. Beatrice had never watched her make it beginning to end, but remembered it involved a marrow and bone base. You couldn't go wrong with soup.

Soup was good.

She took a taxi to Balducci's, and bought three large beef bones, an onion, and carrots. She could not remember what other vegetables went in. Something green, leafy. Escarole? Maybe it had been collard greens. She bought bunches of both. And peas — peas sounded right. She got a loaf of peasant bread, a stick of sweet butter, and a quart of green olives. Cyril was crazy for green olives. Pickles too. He loved pickles. She bought a gallon jar of pickles. On the way home, she stopped at the liquor store down Sixth Avenue and bought two bottles of red wine and a bottle of Teacher's. That should cover them.

As soon as she got back to the loft, she put an apron on and went to work. Unanswerable questions immediately arose. Did one bring the water to boil and then add the bones? How long did the bones have to cook? Did one sauté the vegetables first or throw them in raw? Her heart was racing. There was hardly any meat attached to the bones. Maybe one was supposed to buy some extra meat, separately. Maybe one bought additional, extracted marrow as well.

She put the largest pot she owned — a pasta pot — on the

stove, threw in the bones, covered them with water, added salt and pepper, and turned the burner on. It could take care of itself for now — no need to watch it, she hoped. She washed the greens, scraped the carrots, and shelled the peas. Each leaf separated and thoroughly washed, the collards and escarole doubled up in volume. It'd be like threading a camel through a needle to fit it all in the pot. Maybe the leaves had to be chopped. That would certainly reduce the bulk. She cut the leaves into pieces one at a time, then chopped the carrots into cubes, aiming for symmetry, though it was hard to imagine how that could be done, seeing as how the stalks were rounded and grossly uneven. She guessed one had to throw out the tapering parts. This done, after deliberating a long time over how to deal with the onion, she decided the safest bet was to grate it.

What else? Nothing else, except the pot had started making a fierce chugging, rattling noise. With extreme caution, for it sounded like a broken-parts, loose-valves engine about to explode, she lifted the lid and peeked in. A frothy, slimy substance, for which she could not conjure another name but "scum," was bubbling blithely through the broth and up the sides of the pot.

She ran to the phone and called home. Without as much as saying hello, she asked her stepmother if she could talk to Mrs. Engle.

"Yes, dear, that happens," Mrs. Engle said in her unflappable, officious voice. "You have to skim it."

"How?"

"With a spoon, dear. You take a large spoon and you skim it."

Beatrice tried to skim it, but the more she skimmed, the more scum rose up. She dropped paper towels in and swiveled them around, which had a somewhat better result, except that it soaked up a lot of the broth as well — a kind of throwing the baby out with the bathwater. Froth was not the worst thing. Many good things made froth — boiled milk, beer.

She took the bones out, scraped the meat off, cut it up in tiny pieces, and threw it back in. Without the bones displacing it upward, the level of the water had sunk down to five inches. She added some more, a lot more. She put the vegetables in, packing in the greens with the expectation they'd shrink. They did. They took their sweet time, but they shrank all right — now looking soggy and a sorry dull green you'd have to close your eyes to eat. Other than that and the fact that the broth did not have the thick texture she remembered, making the vegetables float a bit too unmoored in it, she'd done well. The soup tasted good. Looks shouldn't matter that much — it all turned to mush in the stomach.

It was only two o'clock. There was nothing more to do, but it was making her anxious just to be waiting, doing nothing.

Earlier, as she was taking Ned's clothes out of the closet, she'd come across a raincoat Faye had passed on to her because she'd grown too heavy to wear it. It had cost three hundred fifty dollars, was made of a silky synthetic material that resembled parachute cloth, and had a silvery off-white color, pearl-like in its shine. Though it hung somewhat loose on her, with the belt tied tight it was extremely flattering to her figure, giving her, like Ned said, a sultry Mata Hari–Greta Garbo look — emphasis less on spy than stripper. He used to love her in it, used to make her wear it naked underneath and flash him.

The downside was that it sucked up grime, meshing it into its fibers evenly as dye. She'd stopped wearing it years ago because it had become disgustingly, utterly filthy and could not be dry-cleaned or machine-washed but had to be washed by hand, which she'd put off and put off, till she'd forgotten it still hung in the closet.

As luck would have it, its time had come. She filled the sink with warm soapy water, threw it in, and went at it with manic fervor. The dirt wouldn't come off.

She called Faye. "Can't chat right now," she said fast. "That raincoat you gave me? I'm trying to wash it, and nothing happens."

"Try a toothbrush," Faye said.

"A toothbrush?"

"Yeah. And toothpaste. It gets out anything."

Beatrice tried the toothbrush on the darkest spot. The dirt lifted up, curling like gummy adhesive, but it wouldn't slough off. She had to pick it off with her nails. It was a painstaking and extremely slow process — soothing at first, but after half an hour she had cleared just a small patch by the hem, her hand was hurting from gripping the toothbrush furiously tight, her forearm was shaking and now, suddenly, her whole body started to shake. She was coming apart at the seams over a fucking filthy raincoat. *What am I doing?* she thought. *What am I doing! What if the dumb thing cost three hundred and fifty dollars!*

Would she slave over it if it cost a thousand? Ten thousand? A hundred thousand? No! For a million dollars, she wouldn't do it. She hoisted the raincoat out of the sink, put it in a plastic bag, soapy wet as it was, and took it out of the loft, leaving it by the door. Out of her life! Begone! It had been touch-and-go there for a while. She'd thought she might be losing her mind. The opposite: it had been a proof of her sanity and a boost to her faith — a shaking fit by the kitchen sink, her road-to-Damascus, ha-ha, moment. Money was just barter. It held no candle to the essence of things. It was what she'd always believed. She didn't know what had come over her, not throwing the raincoat in the garbage the moment she saw the dirt wouldn't come out. It wasn't like her. Nothing she did was like her for days now, for months — hell, years.

She uncapped the Teacher's, brought it over to the table, and sat at a chair. If she were to use a glass, she'd have to keep count. No stops and measures for Ms. Trix — no sirree! Trixie knew how to get her kicks. Welcome to the funhouse! The mood roller-coaster — steepest in all the West and East. Get a free ride! Cheap thrills! Southern Comfort the Teacher's wasn't, but to each his taste.

She stacked her Janis Joplin records on the record changer and turned it on.

Down on me, lord, down on me . . .

She sang along, rocking from side to side in a lulling motion. It didn't take long for the alcohol to mellow her out. Maudlin was good. It was just one step from maudlin to "see if I care."

She turned the volume up high. Only music could fire up the passion of emotions smoldering in us, only music fully answered our yearning. It was slow-burn, or sing . . . slow-burn, or dance . . . Janis was the real thing.

She drank and danced, holding the bottle in her hand. Never in her life had she danced with such abandon, such devil-may-care sexy swank. She kicked her shoes off. She messed up her hair. She undid the clasp of her necklace and tied the stringed pearls like a loose belt around her hips. She turned up the volume all the way.

> Bye, bye-bye, baby, bye-bye
> I guess I'm gonna make it okay
> I'll see you in the funny papers some old day
> Bye, bye-bye, baby, bye-bye

While Cyril was away in Vietnam, Ned had taken Beatrice home to meet his parents on a two-day, one-night visit. He had slept in his old room; Beatrice had been given Cyril's, a small narrow room with a sole window at the far end, a single bed, a chest of drawers, a shelf covered with his trophies, and nothing else. The window, the walls, the floor were bare, the air was stale and thick with dampness, the mattress sagged, and the sheets and blankets smelled of mold and something indefinably rank, akin to wet dog fur. Later, when Ned sneaked in and lay down next to her, the smell seemed to come off his body. She went numb. All she wanted was to have the bad odor go away so she could smell Ned's skin — be able to hold him, to just hold him. He forced her to have sex. It was the first time he had been rough with her, and she took it as fair punishment for being revolted by the air he had been breathing his whole young life. After she came, while he still kept at it, she was unable to get it out of her mind that they were on his brother's bed. That very moment, he might be lying wounded or dying.

Back in New York, Ned was gentle again. She was happy with him — things hadn't taken a downward turn yet — but now her happiness seemed stolen from the dead. She had no right to it, she thought, while men were still being slaughtered over there.

She had had no idea what Cyril looked like. There had been no framed photos on display at the house — none of Ned, nor the parents themselves either. She had nothing to go by, for Ned refused to talk about him. The one time she asked him pressingly what he was like, he said: "A head taller than me, heavyset."

"As a person, I mean."

"He thinks he's always right."

Both his silence and his tone made it clear that the two had not gotten along and that Ned held a grudge against Cyril, even hated him. By then, he had come to personify her guilt about the war, and the fact that Ned didn't seem to care his brother might get killed helped to increase her empathy. She imagined Cyril as honorable and brave, dutiful to a fault — everything that Ned was not. In her fantasies, he had Ned's features, somewhat blurry, and in most of them he was wounded and she was nursing him back to health.

He proved to be nothing like she'd imagined. Ned had

spoken the truth. Cyril did think he was always right, but that was the one thing that bothered her least. It was hard to accept the drug dealing, the company he kept, the bar fights, the silent, daunting way he watched people, the blunt manner in which he spoke, not bothering to hear out what others had to say, as if it didn't matter or it bored him. He was profoundly sad, which showed only at moments when he was sitting around exhausted, a cigarette burning away between limp fingers, his eyes unfocused. Otherwise, his face had an arrogant, blatantly righteous expression. She saw all that but it made little dent in her feelings. She liked him. There was real substance and strength in him, she thought, an apparent integrity and sense of valor. Something at the core of his being other than character, personality, or temperament — something that was impossible to define — made her feel he was blood.

In that profound sense, Ned had always seemed "other." It was, perhaps, why in the beginning — for months — it had been so hard to spend a single moment apart. The feeling of otherness had been threatening and scary, like a secret weapon they each carried, which at a distance came to the fore but hid from sight at close range. There was no such insecurity and mistrust between her and Cyril.

At this point, it should be a gliding step from friendship to sex, yet she was terrified to take it. She felt as if she'd be playing her last card, folding a losing hand.

On Cyril's part, it had been love at first sight, and trying to smother his desire for her had only made his love stronger. So far, he had toed the line. Now that Ned had left her, and especially after her phone call today, he was ready to act on his feelings.

At this moment, he was standing outside her door. He had been banging on it with his fist for over ten minutes and was now considering kicking it in. When she finally opened it — in the silent break between one record coming to an end and the next one dropping down — he was standing with his right hand raised in a fist, about to pound the door again, and his left arm hanging at his side, a long-stemmed white calla lily upside down in his hand, held as if he were wielding a club. He was in a suit and tie, his hair greased and combed back, sticking compactly to his skull.

"I've been dancing," she said smiling, but vaguely, at him. "Wanna dance?"

The music had resumed at full blast. The bass was making the floorboards and the air vibrate as if a tornado were about to touch down.

"Turn it off!"

She walked to the stereo and switched it off. When she turned around, he was still standing by the door.

"I don't think I've ever seen you in a suit," she said.

"I had to groom up for the bank."

"Groom up . . ."

He walked to the table and laid the lily down on it. They both stared at it, then looked away — Cyril, at Beatrice's dressed-to-kill outfit, her harsh makeup, the wanton pain in her eyes; Beatrice, around the floor for her shoes. She found them and put them on. She smoothed her hair, pushing it behind her ears, and tried to untie the knot in the pearls around her waist, but couldn't undo it.

"I guess I'm stuck with it," she said. "Ah, well . . ."

He was standing by the table, an unlit cigarette pressed

tightly between his lips. If he tried to light it, his hands might start trembling from nervousness, from conflicted desire, from anger — whatever was now making them limp at the joints. He tended to rely entirely on instinct, and now his instincts were straggling silent amidst loud, confused emotion. He felt anything but what he had expected he'd be feeling, what he wished to be feeling.

"That's the suitcase — all his things," she said, pointing. "It's not heavy. I can carry it out. Some of the paintings are too big. You'll have to help me."

He took off his jacket, tie, and shirt, draped them over the back of a chair, pulled his T-shirt loose out of the waistband of his slacks, and walked toward the racks.

"You want a drink first?"

He did not answer.

"Did you hear me?"

"I heard you."

He refused her help with the larger paintings but let her carry the smaller ones out. They went back and forth from the storage racks at the end of the loft to the hall outside, without speaking, avoiding each other's eyes.

"I need a hammer to get the nails out," he said, when they were done.

She started to walk toward the kitchen.

"Tell me where it is," he said. "I'll get it."

"Under the counter, by the fridge."

As he was pulling the first nail out, she came up behind him, carrying a wastebasket.

"What's that?" he said.

"A wastebasket."

"I see," he said. "Why are you holding it?"

"For the nails."

"I see," he said again.

She stayed right next to him, lifting the wastebasket under his arm each time he pulled out a nail.

"Put it down, Bea. Put it down, and go sit down."

She sat down on the sofa. It made her too nervous sitting still. In a moment she got up and turned the music back on.

"Turn it off," he yelled. "You want me to do this, turn it off!"

He carried the loose lumber out in the hall, then to the ground floor — five flights, up and down, four trips.

"Do you have a box?" he said, as he came back in.

"What kind of a box?"

He pointed to the wastebasket. "To keep the nails in."

"What would I keep them for? What am I going to do with a bunch of bent nails?"

"They aren't badly bent," he said. "You could use them."

"What for?"

"Whatever for. They're good metal. You don't throw out good metal." He looked away from her. "Now, I'll have that drink."

She poured him a scotch and sat back down on the sofa, taking the bottle along. Cyril sat at the table, on the chair he always sat on when he stayed for dinner but this time uncomfortably, close to the edge. He had an imposing bearing, and unease lay awry over his body. His gruff, irritable side — the way he'd been with her since he walked in — Beatrice was familiar with; not so with this cowed, sulky manner. He wouldn't look her in the eye.

"Are you hungry?" she asked.

"Only had breakfast."

She lit the burner under the pot to reheat the soup.

"I've made soup," she said. "We'll have soup and bread and wine."

She put two place mats on the table — one in front of Cyril, the other directly across from him — and moved the lily so that it lay parallel, equidistant between. She brought the bread, the butter, two spoons, and two wineglasses and placed them down symmetrically. Last, she set two silver candlesticks with white candles on either side of the lily. She lit the candles and stepped back to judge the effect.

"We're all set," she said. "You can open the wine."

He had pushed his chair in and was sitting with his elbows on the table, forearms crossed, head bent.

"You look like you're praying," she said.

"Bea, I'm hungry."

"Well, yes," she said primly. "Now, this is going to look strange, but it tastes good, and it's real good for you."

Soup bowls would be too small. She didn't want to have to get up for refills. She wanted the dinner to run as at a restaurant, both of them sitting down, eating and drinking. Considering a range of possibilities, including filling up six bowls and setting them on the table at once, she decided to use her Pyrex mixing bowls.

"You'll have to forgive the plate," she said, setting the first bowl on Cyril's place mat.

"What is this?" he said.

The clear glass let light through, making the soup broth look like dirty dishwater swimming with grease spots, bits of scrunched-up meat, pieces of carrot, and five or six peas. The greens were floating on the surface like flat-leaf slimy seaweed.

"The way I made it, it doesn't have a name, but in essence it's beef-bone soup."

"Why don't we go out," he said. "I'd like to take you out."

"It's good soup. I've tasted it and it's good. Don't you believe me? Why are you looking at me like this?"

"I believe you," he said, shaking his head. "I believe you. That's what's killing me — I believe you."

"Killing you . . ."

He got up.

"No, no!" she said. "Sit down. I know what to do. I'll put it in the blender. It's the consistency that's wrong. I'll puree it."

There was such intense, frantic despair in her eyes, the rest of her face looked lifeless.

"Have a pickle. I forgot I bought pickles for you."

She handed him the pickle jar. She brought out the olives in their tall quart container.

"I bought them for you. Have them!" she said. "I know you like them, eat them!"

Suddenly, tears began running from her eyes.

Cyril walked up to her and tried to touch her face, but she pushed him away.

"I'm all right," she said. "I'm all right! This is nothing. It will pass."

She poured the soup into the blender, while he stood at her side.

"It will only take a second. It will be good. Have faith!"

She pressed the puree button.

"That's enough time," he shouted.

"You think?"

She lifted the lid and looked down at the soup. It had taken on the greenish brown color and texture of runny shit.

"It only looks bad," she said, putting her finger in and scooping up a smear. She licked her finger. "It's good."

She put her finger back in, scooped up a glob, and brought her finger near his lips. Cyril held her hand hesitantly a moment, then opened his mouth and pushed her whole finger in. Licking it, sucking it, he pulled her tightly to him.

"Cyril . . ."

Her voice was a gentle quake in the pit of his soul, his rising cock. He could feel her soft against him, breathing fast, then her body becoming tense.

"I love you, Bea."

She pulled away.

"How *can* you?"

"You know I love you. Don't force me to say hokey things."

Looking at him and shaking her head, she walked backward with small steps, stopped when she was seven, nine feet away.

"You don't know me," she said. "You don't know me!"

"I know you. It's what frightens you. I know you. You and I are alike."

He tucked his T-shirt into his pants, put his shirt and jacket back on, folded his tie into his right jacket pocket, and took a swill off the wine bottle.

"Put on a coat, and let's go get something to eat," he said.

As they went out the door, he saw the plastic bag that had the raincoat in it and picked it up to take it down to the garbage. He went down the stairs first, and she followed a few steps behind. The water had drained off the raincoat to the bottom of the bag and was making a loud, sloshing noise.

"What's in this thing?" he said.

"A wet raincoat."

He stopped midstep, one foot about to touch down.

"Did it . . . rain today?"

"No."

He started down the stairs again at a faster pace, keeping his head down. By the time he was on the ground floor, she was nearing the second-floor landing. He threw the bag in the garbage and walked back to the bottom of the stairs. She was standing stock-still midway down the last flight.

"About the raincoat," she said. "I can explain."

"Please don't!"

"You think I'm crazy, don't you?"

"Get down, Bea."

"You think I'm fucked-up. Say it!"

"I said, get down!"

He walked to the front door and waited for her there.

She climbed down the stairs. He held the door open, keeping his back to her.

"Where are we going?"

"I don't know where we're going," he said, without turning around.

"We don't have to do it — go out to dinner, I mean."

She touched him under his right shoulder. His muscles tightened, shrinking away from her hand, but in the second she'd touched him, she had felt his heat and the skin on her palm stinging like her blood was ice.

◆

Blue Tit was the place of the moment to be seen. The side room was a world apart from the in-crowd around the bar in the main room, though here too everyone had, or affected, the glutted, gloating look in the eye that spells fame, if not fortune. It was in the side room that Beatrice and Cyril were sitting — Beatrice bedraggled in her evening gown, her hair Medusa-wild and her eyes glaring wide; Cyril stiff like a lumberjack in a brand-new suit, his hair neatly combed back, his eyes half shut. He was sinking deeper and deeper into himself, down to a numbness of all emotion, while his senses remained on high alert. He didn't know what Beatrice might do next. All evening he had been walking on eggshells. Were she any other woman, he would have slapped her on the face. She had been asking for it, like a child out of control. But love unmanned him, he thought — love unmanned him, and without love he was half a man. There you had it.

"You start," she said.

He looked at her.

She had ordered sautéed calf's liver, a double order of the bacon and onions, an extra side dish of mashed potatoes, and creamed spinach instead of string beans. Now that her food was here, she was looking at it with distaste.

"I've lost my appetite. The idea of chewing, swallowing down — can't get into it."

He cut into his steak.

"You should get something in your stomach."

"I've had some bread." She lifted her wineglass, as if

to toast him. "Bread and wine. For the French poor, it's a meal."

He did not respond, other than stooping his head and shoulders closer to his plate, in the manner a jittery driver might bend over the wheel.

"Blue Tit," she said. "I've never heard the expression. It answers 'blue balls,' I guess."

"It's a bird, Bea."

She opened her mouth to say "oh," but instead hiccupped in an endless, stuttering burst.

"You should try and scare me."

"You're drunk."

"It's just the hiccups."

Trying not to look at her, he stuffed large chunks of potatoes and meat in his mouth, hell-bent to get the meal over with and get out.

There'd been a hiatus in the music. Now, as he was putting the last bit of food in his mouth, "Sympathy for the Devil" started playing in the jukebox.

"I love the Rolling Stones," she said. "You?"

Cyril signaled to the waitress to bring the check.

"You?" Beatrice said again.

He just looked at her.

"Ah, we're now playing the silent game," she said.

She swayed her head to the beat. "We've danced to this. Remember?"

"Must have been someone else."

She let that go by, and sang to him with taunting eyes: "Ooo who who . . . ooo who who . . . oh yeah . . . what's my name . . ."

Suddenly, bending forward, she put her hand over his.

"I'll be back," she said. "Got to pee."

"Careful!"

The pearl necklace around her waist had gotten snagged on the corner of the table. She was too far gone to hear him in time. The pearls went flying, rolling, all over the floor, just as a busboy carrying a tray filled with dirty glasses went by. He slipped on the pearls and fell. Without missing a beat, Beatrice made her way among the glass shards and puddles of spilled liquor to the end of the room. *Accidents happen,* she thought. Life was full of accidents. The Big Bang was an accident. Yeah . . . We were all here by accident. Yeah . . .

She turned around and shouted: "I'll be back in a jiffy!"

She blushed from head to foot. Jiffy? Where had *that* come from? Jiffy! Who ever said "jiffy" anymore? Some tight-ass pretentious moron, that was who.

It made it too embarrassing to walk back through the room after she peed. She stood against the wall and made signs with her right hand and arm, then both arms, for Cyril to meet her outside, looking — God help her — like a baseball coach who'd just suffered a stroke and didn't yet know it. If Cyril understood, he did not signal back. He just sat there, gawking. Perhaps all she needed to do was walk out and he'd get the message. But she'd left her purse and coat on the seat. She signed to him to get them for her. What was the matter with him — had he never played charades? He was letting her carry on like a hopeless idiot. Everyone had turned their heads to stare at her. Waitresses were standing about here and there — pillars of salt, like so many wives of Lot. She wouldn't budge till he got it into his head he should come to her.

She stayed completely still — well, except for weaving a bit — and stared at him. See who played chicken better.

Cyril waited till he'd paid the bill then walked over. From up close, he could see she was scared—he could feel her fear, could smell it on her breath. It eased him.

"It'll be all right, Bea."

He put his arms around her, but she pushed him violently away.

"I should have passed a hat," she said, when they were outside. "For the show."

"Talk to me, Bea."

"I think it was funny," she said, laughing hysterically. "It was funny!"

He waited silently till she calmed down.

"Let's go."

He tried to help her with her coat.

"I can do it, thank you," she said. "I don't know about you, but I'd like to go back on foot. I need the exercise. See?"

She opened the flaps of her coat to show him.

He had noticed earlier that she had gained a little weight and had thought nothing of it. Now, the way she rubbed her hand over her stomach made him ask, "Could you be pregnant, Bea?"

"No!"

She denied it as fiercely as she had been trying to deny it to herself. She'd had her period! True, it had lasted only two days and the color of the blood had been brownish like the dregs at a period's end, but blood was blood.

"Why is everyone asking me that? It pisses me off."

She started to cry.

"You can tell me," he said. "It's all right."

"It's not all right. Nothing is all right."

She walked on ahead of him. He followed silently a step behind.

When they came to the door of her building, he took her pearls out of his pocket.

"I hope I got them all," he said.

She looked at them like she did not know what they were. He had gone down on his hands and knees to retrieve them while she was in the bathroom, and she did not even remember she'd lost them.

"I don't want them."

He put the pearls back in his pocket.

"They can be restrung," he said. "I'll do it for you."

She did not respond.

"I assume they're real."

"You assume right. Keep them."

"I'll save them for you," he said.

"You keep them, I don't care. I don't care! I don't care! I don't care!"

"You care, Bea." He looked like he wanted to kiss her, but it was only in the eyes. Both hands were in his pockets. "You need to get some sleep."

"Right."

He went away, walking slowly with his head bent like a man talking to himself. He had not waited to see her safely in the door, and Beatrice lingered outside a moment longer, watching him go. He continued to walk slowly, head low. Suddenly, a cat shot out from under a parked car and he almost fell down, but he righted himself without much wavering, then, chin up, back ramrod-straight, he turned the corner at a brisker pace.

Right.

She climbed up the stairs, fearing she might faint from exhaustion. Nevertheless, as soon as she entered the loft, she became manic. She cleared the table, washed the dishes, scrubbed the counters and the sink, and went back to the table to wipe it clean. What to do with the lily? It had begun to fade already. She should have put it in water right away — would have, if Cyril had handed it to her, but he'd laid it down on the table as on a bier.

Here lies . . . hear lies . . .

You can reuse bent nails . . . you don't throw out good metal.

Flowers were only good while they bloomed.

Sooner or later she'd have to throw it in the garbage. *Do it now*, she thought. *Get it over with.* She started hyperventilating. She wouldn't — couldn't — do it. She'd let it desiccate — set it down on the windowsill where it would get direct sunlight. In the end, everything crumbled, everything became dust, but let beauty die out in dignity, let love for it last.

After carefully dusting the sill of the window that got the most sun, she laid the lily down on it, turning the curled tip of the corolla toward the room and the stamens poking through the fluted single petal away.

APRIL

I sabel, Beatrice's maternal grandmother, maintained an apartment in Paris where she lived most of the year. After her daughter's death, she had fought her son-in-law for sole custody of her grandchild. She had no legal right and her only recourse was to prove him an unfit father on account of his inadequate income and youth. He was nineteen at the time. The year before, he had gone to Paris with some vague idea of becoming a painter. It was there where he had met her daughter, there where she had died bringing Beatrice into the world. A month later, he had gone back to the States, taking his infant child with him.

He and Isabel had never gotten along, and the court battle caused an irreparable rift. After he won, he refused to let her see Beatrice at all. Isabel did not relent. In the end they came to an agreement: she would set up a trust fund for the child and in return would be allowed to have Beatrice for six months in the spring and summer, on the condition she wouldn't take her out of the country.

In addition to the apartment in Paris, she had a house in the south of France. She bought land in Vermont to give

Beatrice a permanent place where she could come stay. It had been a whimsical choice: she had fancied the notion of owning a hill in an area that was rural, unfashionable, and unspoiled. At first she'd thought to build the house like a two-story log cabin, then in quasi-Victorian style, reminiscent of Hansel and Gretel. In the end, she went for Gothic — a gray stone, turreted structure like a small castle. She was fifty-five at the time, recently divorced from her third husband and living with an Irishman, twenty years younger, who professed to be a psychic and used to run séances.

Isabel wasn't a stupid woman, if at times foolish. When she was played, it was with her eyes half open. She bore no grudge against her husbands and all the lovers who'd used her. "Bitterness is the spice of loneliness," she liked to say; but if she felt bitter, she hid it well. She had uncommon dignity and grace. She was also eccentric, egotistical, and vain. She had squandered a fortune indulging her whims and almost an equal amount acting out of noblesse oblige.

She had grown up in Cincinnati, the oldest of six children and the only daughter, and had had modest beginnings — a fact she liked to boast of. Her father had owned a factory that manufactured farming equipment. It was just beginning to flourish before the crash of '29 but had survived, if barely, the depression. Isabel had been well into her twenties when, under the management of her oldest brother, the business expanded into building threshing machines and tractors that, in time, sold around the world.

Like her apartment in Paris and the villa in the south of France, the Vermont house was furnished with an indeterminable taste for austere, stately antiques and cozy comfort.

There was an old-world feeling to it, of clutter, dark up-holstery, and musty air that created a claustrophobic effect, much like a stage set behind the closed curtain. There was, in fact, a theatrical aspect to her life, as of a play whose spirit has been dulling with the run.

As a child Beatrice hated spending time with her. The perennial guests, a social mishmash — Isabel had gone through a brief period of calling herself a communist and took pride in moving in the fringes of the bohemian world — were mostly in their fifties and sixties. Evenings, Bea was made to wear an array of starched white organdy dresses Isabel had bought for her in Paris, or fanciful custom-made outfits based on exotic native costumes, and to sit silently on a wing chair with a small footstool under her feet. She was, she was told, a little princess, and little princesses had to learn to sit straight and still and smile prettily and not show whatever it was they were thinking. Grandma had been made to do the same thing when she'd been young, and it'd done her no harm. It was good discipline, at any rate — not to mention it gave you good posture.

During the day she was given free rein, but no children were among the guests. She spent most of her time at the caretaker's house down the slope. He had a girl her age, a thin sturdy child with a ruddy complexion and a common, rather bland, pretty face, which, when she smiled, lit up with a soon-to-fade, singular beauty like a wildflower's, plucked from a blooming field.

Her name was Maggie, and in personality and manner she was uncannily similar to Faye. Beatrice had been close to her when they were small, but by eleven all Maggie talked about was boys. The confidences went one way and gave Beatrice goose bumps of revulsion. She had no boyfriends herself, and no comprehension of sex. She was aghast when, at twelve, trying to allay her disbelief and disgust that there could be such an act as cunnilingus, Maggie pointed out to her that dogs licked each other's ass and would not do it unless they liked the taste. At fifteen, she told her that blow jobs took practice and come went down in one gulp like raw egg white — a breeze once you got the hang of it. By then Isabel was paying Maggie to help around the house along with her mother, who came in regularly to clean. Maggie seemed to get fatter and coarser by the day — also meaner.

The meanness had been there all along, sudden bursts that took Beatrice too much by surprise for her to feel hurt. There was one exception, when they were six.

It had been late afternoon, a rainy day. They had been rolling in a puddle of mud, pasting mud on each other, the face, the hair, caressing tenderness hidden under each soiled touch. Beatrice was lying on her back, laughing from fun, when Maggie suddenly thrust a handful of mud into her open mouth. Beatrice jumped to her feet, gagging. The mud was smeared on her tongue and the inside of her mouth, too thickly stuck to swallow or spit out. She burst out crying. But it wasn't the mud in her mouth that had made her cry. It was the gleam of malice in Maggie's eyes, her little satisfied smile, as she kept staring at her.

"Crybaby," she said. "Crybaby!"

Back at the house, the French nanny gave her a bath, muttering as she scrubbed her, "*Comme un cochon . . . comme un cochon . . .*" Afterward, she dressed her in a bright green, red, and gold sari, hung a sapphire pendant over her forehead, and covered her head with a lacy silver veil.

She was made to wait shut in her room for punishment till cocktail time, when she had to endure an hour perched in her chair — the pretty granddaughter on display.

"Low company will bring you low," Isabel said to her the next morning. "You're too young to understand this now, but love is like water: it always rises to its level, making what's more less. It's the better person who's always the loser."

She forbade her to play with Maggie again, and Beatrice stayed home that day, but the next day she stole out of the house to go be with her. She had run all the way through the woods, to the end of the path. Maggie was out in her yard but pretended not to see her. Beatrice sidled up to her like a kicked dog and suffered in silence till Maggie said, "Last one to the road is a rotten egg."

After she started grammar school, her stay in Vermont was limited to July and August, and her father became the main center of her emotional world.

He was a retiring, melancholy man. It was as if his one act of rebellion — fleeing to Paris and marrying for love — had sapped his will to strive further. He joined the family business, which was tea imports, and lived with his parents till they died in a car crash, seven years after he had returned from Paris. Within weeks of his parents' death, he married a divorced woman considerably older than he was. On her insistence, they moved into the house her ex-husband had settled on her, uprooting Beatrice without much notice.

He had three more children from his second marriage, all boys. He was remote with them. He was remote with his second wife. He let her run things, and treated her with courtesy, bearing her strident, domineering manner with icy reserve. He claimed to have remarried for Beatrice's sake and he believed it, but he was remote with her as well. He traveled frequently on business while she was small, and paid her little attention when he stayed home. Nevertheless, he brought back gifts for her from every trip without fail. Most of them were still in the closet of her room back home — dozens of toys and dolls, intact in their boxes. There had been no need to take them out and play. She already had them in duplicate: presents Isabel mailed every few weeks from around the world, or bought by him on previous trips.

The sole times he suffered her to show him her affection were when he handed her a gift and bent his head down for a kiss, offering her the lower edge of his cheek, where the skin was hard-grained with stubble and chafed against her child-soft lips. That tingling itch, she had thought, was what love was like — that, and waiting anxiously for him to come back from each trip, up in bed, if he arrived late at night.

When she reached her teens and her resemblance to her mother started becoming more pronounced, if she caught him unawares, coming upon him suddenly and startling him, for a second his eyes would light up with love; then, as he looked away from her, she could see, blatant on his face, disappointment and grief. He had adored her mother, and in Beatrice he saw the cause of her death, perhaps; or it was the fact that, though she had inherited her mother's beauty, she was nothing like her otherwise, and whatever lay beneath her appearance was unworthy of his love or even a longer look. Her success at school, her various accomplishments seemed to leave him unmoved.

The only memento she had of her mother was a music box her grandmother had given her when she was nine, telling her that her mother used to have one just like it and she had searched heaven and earth to find one for Beatrice to have. It was made of rosewood inlaid with ivory and gold leaf in a geometric design, too simple to appeal to a child, and Beatrice had stared at it with disappointment — and shock, that heaven and earth had been searched for a plain box. It wasn't the same one her mother had once held in her hands. What good was it to touch it, a false thing, a copy? When she had opened it, it played *"Eine Kleine Fruhlingsweise."* She had adored the melody at first, but it made her sad to play it, for it just ended — abruptly — and she didn't want it to ever end. Playing it over only made it end again, and it was like sucking candy that, just as it began to taste sweetest, turned into a pebble, a cold stone in her mouth she couldn't spit out.

She had not known love as a child. It had been a hankering for love that had bound her to Ned. Now, he had abandoned her, but she believed she still loved him. The despair she felt was love shorn naked, she thought — love skinned alive.

Without a job to go to, without obligations or a structure of any kind, one day flowed indistinguishably into the next. Nothing was defining her life. In the empty immensity of the loft even her solitude lacked a center. The bare walls were pitted with nail and thumbtack holes where Ned had hung his canvases and pinned up his drawings. All his traces were gone but these holes, and the huge mark where the painting racks had stood. The floor there was shiny and smooth as it had been right after it had been sanded and varnished, yet the eye went to it as to a smudge.

Like a long mantra, she kept repeating silently in her mind a verse from the Old Testament that she had started repeating to herself day in, day out, when she first realized her marriage was descending into hell: *I shall have peace, though I walk in the imagination of mine heart, to add drunkenness to thirst.*

The imagination of mine heart . . .

What was it she imagined, really?

Her thoughts were muddled, her feelings were muddled: it was like trying to get to solid ground through quicksand.

She spent the last three weeks of March going over her notes on Kierkegaard and Weil, thinking she might be able to salvage her thesis and perhaps turn it into a book. *The Wish/The Hunger* . . . male/female . . . get to the point where their ideas merge: Kiekegaard's belief that truth is what ennobles and Weil's that love is not consolation but light. If she could only fully grasp this! She had a vague intuitive understanding but couldn't bring her reason to bear on it. With "truth is what ennobles" she could see her way through, but with "love is not consolation" she couldn't. If love wasn't consolation, no consolation was possible in this life.

She tried rereading their books, hoping it would help her understand.

Whereas years ago she'd read Kierkegaard with excitement and complete absorption, now it was like listening to a solemn piece of music perpetually repeated. He merely mesmerized her. Perhaps because he had written prolifically — some of his work, as his sermons, seemingly by rote — he often sounded peeved and obdurate, like a man with a chip on his shoulder. Simone Weil seemed to be the gentler, purer soul, and rereading her work was easier, for Beatrice could still respond to Weil's mysticism, though she recoiled at the dogmatic, religious underpinning of Weil's thought. Mysticism begged the question, when it didn't let go the strictures of organized faith. The fact that Simone Weil had converted to Catholicism made her especially suspect: one couldn't blame the unconscious effect of outgrown, yet tenaciously rooted, catechetical beliefs.

At last, Beatrice understood what really set her teeth on edge while reading them. It was their acceptance of Christianity's belief in an afterlife. Belief in another world weakened any faith in this one, and the implicit, inherently pessimistic rejection of this life was anathema to her. The Christian creed rejected in essence, she thought, all physical aspects of reality. It rejected the body itself.

If there was a God, she thought, it was the physical world that proved His existence. Life was a miracle whether there was or wasn't an afterlife. A lowly leaf of grass growing from a windswept seed was miracle enough and proof that the universe was holy. If dead leaves of grass were to fill out with sap again and breathe, would that then prove it holier?

In the end, Christ had died peacefully on the cross. To imagine that His spirit, after His last agony of doubt, had not regained strength — to imagine that in His last moments He abnegated the truth He had preached and lived by, believing His body would rise from the dead — was to deny the meaning and example of His sacrifice.

He had said, "The kingdom of God is within you."

On April 1, she put her thesis aside and decided to make a fresh start, turning to her own work. She should try to write fiction, she thought. She should try to write a story about her evening with Cyril — four parts: "Wet Raincoat in a Bag," "Shit Soup," "Floorshow of the Hapless Mime," and "Saving the Lily."

She spent the next two weeks writing it. Sentences would come to her, just the way poetry lines used to come — a silent voice in her ear, in this instance jaunty, arch, ironic, hysterically funny. She had cut a ridiculous figure, but laughing at herself first meant laughing last. Beatrice Redux, she thought — from aspiring poetess to jester. So much for thinking there was more to life than met the eye . . . so much for believing a life worth dying for was the only life worth living. To hell with any heroic or mystical vision. To hell with her old lyrical voice. The tongue-in-cheek was a bloody sword back in its sheath: irony eviscerated reality. It was kill or be killed, and irony cravenly struck underhand, but it struck first and it struck hard.

Yeah, she'd have the last laugh. She'd finally found her real voice.

When she completed the story and read it over, it had her in stitches. She laughed so hard she cried. She laughed so hard her body went into convulsions and her diaphragm hurt as if she'd been kicked in the stomach. A little fit of hysteria, she thought—all was well on the home front. "Hysterical," from the Greek *hysterikos*, meant "of the womb." Hysteria: a woman's realm. Her whole life, she'd been flying high in no-man's-heaven, and now she'd hit the ground, where she belonged.

Nothing more to lose, nothing to live for—Janis's freedom, heroin freedom. It killed you. No one ever died laughing.

Yeah . . . she'd have the last laugh.

But when she read the story a second time, it didn't make her laugh. It wasn't funny; sarcastic, that's all it was. It made her loathe herself. That was perhaps precisely what sarcasm was—self-loathing's glib mask. She had described everything as it had happened, she hadn't lied, yet the story felt like a lie. It wasn't the truth. She could not articulate this in reasoned terms, but self-loathing was a defense against truth—itself a lie. It took a kind of self-love to want to write. It took a kind of pride.

It took—ultimately—she realized, self-love to continue wanting to live. Her writing would amount to nothing, and her life would amount to nothing, till she could own that self-truth, that love.

It was easy enough to honor the part of the insight concerning her writing and say, "I'm not yet ready," and give up. Her writing could wait. She wished she could as easily defer confronting her life. It was too hard, too abstract, her idea of self-love. She could remember her first sense of self when she was little, that wondrous confidence that spells "I," the same in every child. That, she thought, was self-love—what was in everyone innate. That first sense of self, as memory, was quite vivid but did not seem to connect to her present experience of herself.

Yes, it did connect. It was inside her like a hollow reed, which pain made desperately sing, $I-I-I$ . . .

Throughout this whole time, she had not spoken to anyone. She had bought an answering machine to screen her calls but, other than Dyer, no one had called — not Ned, not Cyril, not Faye. Colin had said a grumbly hello the two times she had run into him on the stairs and had seemed eager to avoid her, scrambling away. Perkins, whom she had not seen once since the night of Faye's show, she now saw every day in the hallway or out on the street. Always, he was alone. Always, he looked her hard in the face, then looked away without extending a greeting.

His peacoat open, in a black turtleneck sweater, tight black jeans, and narrow-toe boots, his hair chin-length and greased back without a part, he looked elegant and menacing. The ugliness of his features — a jutting forehead, small, close-set eyes, and a thick-lipped, wide mouth — subsumed in the aura of a strong sexual force, had a compelling appeal. His bearing was arrogant, insidiously aggressive; like a stalking animal, he held his power at bay, seeming to have no qualms, or doubts, about seizing his prey. All this she perceived, but it did not entirely dispel the more romantic view of her first impressions, when he had seemed beyond good and evil, above the strictures of society or fate.

In late afternoon, sometimes late at night, past midnight, boys — two, three, as many as four — would wait outside his door, sitting as Chris had, with their backs leaning against the wall and their legs stretched out. They looked to be in their early teens, and were bedraggled, hollow-cheeked, and sickly pale. The expression of dull hostility in their eyes only hardened if she smiled or said hello.

After she gave up on the story, she spent most of her days drinking. Other than the couple of hours when she passed out cold, she couldn't sleep at night. In darkness, the wall between the two lofts seemed to dissolve, and it was as if nothing separated her from the other side. She believed that no crime was worse than the abuse and exploitation of children, and Perkins's boys were barely out of childhood. Some looked to be no more than thirteen. She had no doubt he sold them drugs and suspected he might be their pimp. In any case, he had sex with them — rough sex, as he had had with Chris. She could hear their screams through the wall.

The existence of pure evil in the world had always been a theoretical idea for her, but she was now feeling it touching her like a tangible force.

Yet, when Perkins came back home near dawn and the light escaping through the transom fell over the area of the floor where the bed had once lain, she was grateful to have him be there. The light was pure, irrespective of its source. The way the luminous contour of its shaft graduated into shade was like a lone sunbeam splitting the clouds on a stormy day. It made her feel less lonely. She would look at it and take heart: truncated by the ceiling and floor, it shone like a ray of hope.

She'd make it through, she thought. Yes, she'd make it through.

BEFORE

She believed it despite the steady, stealthy fear that besieged her: every day, every other day, a single drop of bright red blood stained her underpants. It didn't feel or look like period blood. It was like blood flowing fresh, odorless, from some hidden cut.

D r. Sullivan, a prim, pudgy-cheeked man with white hair in a buzz cut and horn-rimmed glasses, was of an age when a man begins to believe there's little that his eyes haven't seen that would shock him. He was puritanical nonetheless, and not beyond passing moral judgment. He had treated Beatrice three times for VD, all in one year when she was nineteen. When he had cautioned her to be more careful, she said: "Careful? How can one be careful? It's like catching a cold. You do or you don't." In her candid nonchalance, he'd seen mere insolence, far more offensive than the promiscuity itself. Now, at first glance when she walked into his office, he could tell she was pregnant and did not want to have the child. He braced himself.

She had sat down directly opposite him across the desk and was taking deep breaths, clutching her bag tightly in both hands. He waited for her to speak first, not wanting to ease the way. Most women in her situation avoided looking him in the eye. She didn't. It was he who had to look away in the end.

"What seems to be the problem?" he said.

"For three weeks now, I've been bleeding. It's only a drop or two of blood but almost every day."

"When did you have your last period?"

Beatrice tried to remember. "Eight weeks ago."

"What was the date?"

"I don't remember the exact date. Eight weeks ago, give or take a few days."

He looked at the calendar on his desk, counted back the weeks, and noted down the approximate date on her chart.

"It's important to keep track of these things."

"Right."

"Do you have any pain or discomfort?"

"No."

"Let's have a look."

It was six thirty. He waited till Beatrice had gone to the examining room to get undressed, then started phoning back patients who had left messages for him through the day.

Beatrice waited, covered in a white sheet, her legs up in the stirrups.

The examining room was windowless, painted white, longer than wide, and had bright fluorescent lights on the ceiling. It was completely silent, as if sealed off from the living world — an antiseptic portal to sickness and death.

Twenty minutes later Sullivan walked in, with no apology for having made her wait, and went directly to the task ahead, sitting on the small stool and bending between her legs.

The nurse stood silently by.

"Open up wider," he said. "More."

He used the speculum, then examined her with his hand.

"Relax," he said. "You have to relax."

"Is it something bad?" Beatrice said, when he was done. "Could it be cancer?"

Sullivan peeled the gloves off his hands — one, the other — slowly.

"You're right as rain," he said. "You're pregnant."

"I can't be! I've had no sex since my last period."

"You're nine to ten weeks along."

"I've had my period, I just told you. Now I've been bleeding steadily for three weeks."

"Spotting," he said. "That happens. Dress, and come to my office."

He left.

The nurse helped Beatrice get down from the examining table.

"Congratulations," she said in a curt, flat voice.

Beatrice weaved, unsteady on her feet.

"Where is my bag?" she said frantically. "I don't see it. Did I leave it outside?"

"It's under your clothes," the nurse said. "You need to calm yourself, Mrs. James. It's not good for the baby to get so agitated."

She was a matronly middle-aged woman with curly gray hair. A mask of makeup and caked powder gave her eyes a stark intensity without revealing what she was thinking or feeling.

"Let me get you a glass of water," she said. "You stay right there."

She left.

Beatrice put her clothes back on, including her coat, which she buttoned up to the neck. She didn't wait for the nurse.

"Dr. Sullivan," she said, bursting into Sullivan's office, "my mother died in childbirth."

He was making notes on her chart.

"You're not your mother," he said, without looking up. "Everything looks fine."

"How can that be, with the bleeding?"

"You have to forget about the bleeding." He closed her chart, took off his glasses, puffed on the lenses, and dried them with a tissue. "It will stop. You need to take better care of yourself and rest. Will you do that?"

"I don't know . . ." she said. "I've been so unhappy."

"The news hasn't sunk in yet. It will soon make you happy."

He had put his glasses back on and was writing her a prescription.

"This is for vitamins," he said. "You take them twice a day. Make sure you drink enough milk. You should come back to see me in two weeks."

She got up to leave.

"One more thing. You should get your teeth checked. Do you have good teeth?"

"Yes," she said. "Yes, I have good teeth."

She was already at the door, with her back to him, when he called after her, "Sometimes, a good thing happens at a bad time, sometimes, a bad thing at a good time. Of the two, a good thing at a bad time is what you should be wishing and be grateful for."

She hung her head.

"See you in two weeks," he said.

His office was on Seventy-third Street and Park. Beatrice thought she'd get on the subway at Sixty-eighth Street, but she went past it, past Fifty-ninth, Fifty-first, past Grand Central, and kept going, walking so fast her feet pounded the ground seemingly without weight. She was scared. She could feel her heart pounding but no other part of her body, as if she were held together by force of gravity and motion alone. She thought of the night she had conceived — of the absence of love and pleasure in the act — and of Ned leaving her. She thought of her love for him in the early days and how unreal it seemed this moment, how it made everything a lie — a lie, the child. Nothing felt real, that was what scared her the most.

Seventy-three blocks to Washington Square, through the Village down to SoHo, she did not slow her pace.

By the time she reached her neighborhood, it was just past eight in the evening. The factories and businesses were closed, the corrugated metal gates of the stores pulled down and locked, most of the buildings deserted. Only a handful of other people were walking on the streets, and the solitary cars driving by had their long headlights on and were moving slowly as if on a bumpy, narrow road.

She'd never felt this isolated and alone.

A block away from her street, she suddenly turned her face to the right, without knowing what had caught her eye. She found herself staring at the lighted window of a small gallery. There was a single painting on display, a pastel of a rowboat on an empty beach. The sea was calm, the sky clear. The boat stood upright on its keel, the bow barely touching the water's lip. It was painted a weathered gray-white, had no oars, and on its side, by the stern, wide-spaced capital letters in flaky black paint spelled HOPE. Hope abandoned? Hope moored?

The horizon was open, the sea a gleaming soft blue, the sand smooth. The conveyed feeling was at once peaceful and haunting.

The painting and the fact that, though closed for the day, the gallery was lit up proved that fate decreed even the symbolic incidents in life. Everything seemed to be unfolding with the inevitability of a dream, where there was no waking or sleep, her destiny an infinitesimal thread in an infinite weave. Tight in place or unraveled, it had no power to affect the pattern and it hardly mattered what she felt or did.

◆

Chris was covered in blood. The left side of his face was battered, his left eye was swollen shut, and there was a deep gash in his upper lip. He had just come out of Perkins's loft and the door behind him was still open. His face lit up as he saw Beatrice come up the stairs, and he smiled—a wide smile that splayed the cut on his lip and made it bleed into his mouth.

Past his shoulder, Beatrice could see Perkins standing a few feet in from the door, a burning cigarette in his hand, the arm hanging down at his side. She saw him put the cigarette in his mouth, take a deep drag, and blow the smoke out in staggered, widening rings. She heard him say, "Close the door." She saw a boy in a black cowboy shirt and with a shaved head strut to the door and shut it. She saw there was blood splattered on the hallway tiles. She smelled a putrid smell—something like rotten eggs and rotten meat combined. She saw Chris wobbling toward her in slow motion. She saw blood trickling into his mouth. She saw he was smiling at her.

"It's you," he said.

It took her a moment to recover from shock, and then her first reaction was rage.

"Did Perkins do that to you?"

"No . . ."

She put her arms around him.

"What happened?" she whispered, stroking the back of his head. "What happened?"

His hair was sticky with blood. She couldn't see the cut, but it wasn't bleeding; the blood was caked like soft mud.

"You want me to take you to a hospital?"

"No hospital."

"What happened?"

"It's nothing," he said. "It's nothing."

She took him by the hand, and they went into her loft.

"You should wash the blood off. Take a shower."

She turned on the floor lamp by the couch and went to the closet to get him clean clothes. Beatrice was still in a state of shock, though the effect had waned. It seemed a life-or-death decision what she should give him to wear. She took a long time to decide. In the end she picked out a royal blue velour sweat suit and brought it over, together with a white T-shirt, wool socks, a towel, and a washcloth.

"Here."

Chris barely heard her voice. Her face blurred around the edges. He could see it and floating over it, sharper, the image of her face as he remembered it from the first night they met. He closed his eyes, to stay with the feeling, what he had felt then, and all the times he'd thought about her — happiness half-doubted, half-believed like happiness in a dream, the only happiness he'd felt since he didn't know when. Why was it so dark? His eyes were closed, that was why. He opened them, and it was still dark. The windows looked like black mirrors. There were dead flies all over the walls, pinned like butter-flies.No, it was holes. There were small holes in the walls — buckshot holes. Someone had scatter-gunned her walls.

"Chris?"

He looked at the clothes and towels in her hands but didn't reach out to take them, so she walked to the kitchen and set them on the counter near the shower stall.

"Here," she said.

When she turned around, he had taken off his jacket and was struggling, but languidly, to pull his sweater and T-shirt off at one go.

Beatrice watched him undress, feeling a shyness she'd never felt with grown men. He had lost weight since she'd last seen him and he had been thin then; he was skin and bones, and his skin was the sickly shade of tallow that dark skin becomes when pale. She noticed the tracks on his arms, but fast. Her eyes went to the right side of his ribs — two large fresh bruises, a livid crimson like the color of his lips . . . his nipples. He had a long thick penis — uncut, which startled her. It was the first one she'd seen.

She looked at it, fast away and back, then down at the floor, and didn't look up again till she heard the shower curtain close.

She was still in her coat. She took it off, went back to the closet to hang it, and waited there. It was like standing on thin, crackling ice — if she didn't move it'd break, if she did it'd break. She was so caught up in trying to keep calm she didn't hear that the water had stopped running.

"Beatrice!"

"I'm here."

He had sat down at the table. His shoulders were slumped against the back of the chair, his arms hanging limp at his sides.

"I thought you were gone," he said.

"Where would I have gone?"

She couldn't see into him. His left eye was swollen shut, the right eye wide open, the pupil constricted like a cat's but to a round point, gleaming with limpid black light. Beatrice didn't know heroin did that. She thought it could be a sign he had suffered a concussion. The only thing she knew about concussions was that the person had to try and stay alert. She thought strong coffee would help.

"I'll go make some coffee."

She put the percolator on the stove and carried the sugar bowl, the creamer, and a spoon to the table, one at a time, going back and forth.

"Chris, you have to tell me if you feel dizzy suddenly."

He didn't feel dizzy. He felt like he was floating under-water, breathing soft bubbles, and the water was getting colder. He was coming down fast.

"Do you feel disoriented?"

He snorted, a sound like an aborted, sneering laugh.

"You could say that."

She put a cup down on the table in front of him. "Sorry — the saucer is broken."

Chris picked up the cup and held it on the palm of his hand. It was feather light. It was like holding nothing — the prettiest cup he'd seen in his life.

"Put it down. Let me pour," she said.

He stirred in four heaping spoonfuls of sugar, raised the cup to his mouth, and took a sip. The piping hot coffee seeped into the open cut on his lip, making him jump to his feet. Coffee had splattered across the table and all over his sleeve, burning his skin. He started to pat his sleeve dry, slapping his forearm with his left hand, each time hitting harder like he was punishing himself.

"Chris, stop it!"

She tried to grab his hand, but he pushed her violently away and she had to force her arms around him, putting all her strength into it, thinking he'd push her away again, but he clutched onto her and started crying — wailing with loud, shuddering sobs. His body was light and limber like a frail child's, and she caressed his back to comfort him. When he became calmer, when the last dry sobs were barely a quiver, she kissed the crook of his neck and held him gently, freezing as she felt him get hard.

"Sorry," he said.

He broke away and stepped back. "Sorry . . . sorry . . . sorry . . ."

"No!" she said, shaking her head. No . . ."

She knelt and touched him, leaned her face against him. "No . . ."

As she tried to take him in her mouth, he reeled.

"Not you," he said. "Not you."

But he didn't push her off. He held her head, softly pressing his fingers through her hair.

They made love on their sides, face to face. As they kissed, the cut in his lip started bleeding again and his blood filled her mouth. She swallowed it, but could still taste it when she came. He couldn't come. In the end, she turned onto her back and he laid his head on her breasts. They stayed like that, Beatrice stroking his hair though it was still wet and her hand was becoming cold.

"Is your name really Chris?"

"Christos. It's Greek."

"You're Greek?"

"My mother was."

"Is she dead?"

He didn't answer. His breathing became labored and fast, and in a moment he lifted his head off her chest and turned to his side, facing away.

"She was sick for two years before she died," he said. "It was like nothing in the end. It was like she was already gone."

Chris's mother had died of cancer. Near the end, she had become so thin even her head shrank. When Chris visited her in the hospital, her eyes were barely open and so glazed over from the drugs it had been hard for him to tell if she could recognize him or not. Then, minutes before she died, her eyes had opened wide, bulging and rolling with fright. She had torn her hospital gown open and sat up, baring her chest. He had been alone in the room with her, too terrified to call for the nurse. The sight of the puckered hollow scars made him sick. He hadn't been able to move. He hadn't been able to speak. She had started to scream, "Na phygēs . . . na phygēs . . ." A nurse had rushed in and had asked him to leave.

"When did she die?" Beatrice asked.

He shivered. Without answering, he closed his eyes.

There had been a bench in the corridor not far from the door — blond wood slats and no back. Someone had left a Styrofoam cup on it. There was a red lipstick stain over the rim — glaring, a paper kiss. He bent his head to see in. It was empty and clean, must have been filled with water. He walked on to the end of the hall and stood by the window, looking out. The cracks on the paved ground were filled with shadow like gushes awash in black blood. Na phygēs . . . you go . . .

"When did she die?" Beatrice asked again.

"Five years ago," he said. "She died when I was eleven."

"I'm sorry." She moved closer, curled her body around him, and folded her right arm over his shoulder. "I'm so sorry."

Her voice sounded far away — floated in the sunlight over the beach. His mother was sitting on the sand with her arms around her knees, she was wearing a straw hat, a white dress with a bright red poppy print — just the flowers, no leaves — red sandals, her toenails were red, there were bruises on her cheek, black stitches on her jaw, she'd put herself between him and his father's fist, no one else was out on the beach, a sailboat pointed toward the Connecticut shore, he wanted to go into the water, he took his shoes off, he was nine years old, she didn't let him go in the water alone, she got up and walked to him, she stood behind him, she put her hand on his head, he wanted long hair like hers, it was cut close to his scalp, he could feel her touch on his skin, she said, you're a good boy, you don't want to worry your mama, she's sick, listen to me, I want to say this now, when you grow up you go back to Greece, *na phygēs, na phygēs*, this is not the real sea, dirty water it is, you've never seen the sea, you've never seen the real sun, you can't be happy here, blood speaks and your blood is Greek . . .

"Do you believe blood speaks?" he said.

She reached for his hand and held it, giving it a soft squeeze. It was cold and clammy and made her feel, with a jolt, the warmth in her own hand, the warmth in her whole body — a sensation of heat dissolving the bounds of her skin. Her love seemed to flow from a place larger than her heart — inside her, outside her, infinite — love that wasn't separate from loneliness but was laced with strength, a love that made her feel sad but peaceful.

It wasn't the "imagination" of the heart, she thought — it was the "knowledge" of the heart. He was a stranger, unknowable in the thoughts of his mind and separate in his body, but she didn't need to know his thoughts or possess his body to love him. True love knew, in silence, to love — because we are all one.

◆

She woke up before him the next morning. Chris was tossing and turning, groaning in his sleep. Beatrice didn't know if he was having a nightmare or if it was the heroin. She didn't know. She didn't know if she should wake him, didn't know how to handle it. She got out of bed, letting him be, but she was scared.

It was past nine, and she'd been in bed over twelve hours. Her body felt heavy and sluggish. She had no appetite but she forced herself to eat a banana and drink a glass of milk.

The phone rang. It was Faye.

"So how about the news, huh?" she said.

Beatrice cupped her hand over the receiver. "What news?" she whispered.

"Why are you whispering?"

"What news?"

"He's there!" Faye said. "Is he there?"

The sudden anger and suspicion in Faye's voice caught Beatrice off guard. It took her a long, silent time to realize she was referring to Ned.

"He isn't here."

"Cyril?" Faye said after a long pause. "Is it Cyril?"

"It's no one you know. What do you want?"

"I thought I'd ask how you felt about the show."

"What show?"

"You don't know?" After a long pause, Faye said in a brusque tone that barely disguised the relish in her voice: "MoMA bought Ned's crow-thing painting, and he's having a one-man show at some new gallery this fall."

"Right."

"I assumed he'd told you."

Beatrice did not respond.

"Are you there?"

"How did you find out? Did he call you?"

"I called," Faye said too casually. "We had dinner a couple of evenings ago. I'm seeing him again tonight."

From the corner of her eye, Beatrice got a glimpse of Chris standing by the bed. She turned to look at him. He had put his underpants on.

"Where is the bathroom?" he said.

Beatrice pointed with the receiver, her arm making a slow arc. She could hear Faye still talking but didn't put the phone back to her ear. When Chris came out of the bathroom, she was still holding it — against her chest. She could feel her jaw start to tremble. He didn't look at her, not one glance in her direction. The swelling over his left eye had spread to his cheek and the side of his nose but the lid was halfway open, the white watery and bloodshot. The other eye was clear but jittery, shifting with an unfocused gaze. He picked up his bloodied clothes and started putting them on with his back to her, his movements unsteady and abrupt, nervously fast.

It wasn't a morning-after distance. It was as if he had become a different person.

"Are you all right?" she asked.

He grimaced and didn't answer.

"Chris, look at me."

He sat down at the table, slumping against the back of the chair as he had the night before, but with his hands on the table, fingertips tapping the wood.

His eyes kept darting to the pack of Pepperidge Farm cookies on the counter.

She brought them to the table and sat down across from him.

"They may be stale."

He ate them one after the other with avid rapidity, no expression showing on his face, as if he couldn't savor, or even experience, the taste.

"I can make you eggs," she said, "if you're still hungry."

He shook his head.

"What time is it?" he said in a moment.

"You have to be someplace?"

"What time is it?" he asked again.

"We need to talk, Chris."

"Later," he said. "Later. What time is it?"

"Nine thirty, quarter to ten . . ."

He got up and started pacing back and forth, five, six steps each way.

"I was thinking . . ." she said. "I have a house in Vermont. We could go. We could go today. We could go right away."

He did not respond.

"Did you hear what I said?"

"Vermont," he said. "You want to go to Vermont."

"I want *us* to go. It will be nice, I promise. It will do you good."

He looked at her, standing still a second. It was too fast — she had only a glimpse of his expression, his face awry with disbelief — and scorn? Something dark. Before she could stand up and stop him, he made for the door.

"Where are you going?"

She stood in the open doorway and watched him silently, helplessly, pound on Perkins's door.

"It's Chris . . . Open up . . . It's Chris . . ." He kept pounding and yelling desperately, then his voice suddenly weakened to a whisper. He stayed his hand limply on the door.

"He must have gone out," she said, lying to protect him, feeling ashamed because she knew he knew it.

She went back inside. He followed her but stopped just in from the door.

"Can you lend me eighty dollars?" he asked. "I'll pay it back."

She jerked to a halt midstride.

"I don't have it."

"I'll pay you back tonight," he said. "I'll have it by midnight."

He walked up and touched her on the shoulder.

She couldn't look him in the eye.

"I'll give it back," he said. "I promise."

She turned to him but still couldn't look him in the eye.

"Look, Chris. I know what you'll use it for. I know what you'll have to do to give it back to me."

"You know nothing," he said. "Forget I asked. I'll get the money elsewhere."

He stared at her with hatred.

"If you go on doing what you do, you'll get killed or die."

He looked away but his face had become sad, softer.

"Do you remember on the street, that night?" he said.

"Yes."

"I thought you wanted me. I thought you were going to pick me up."

"Like a trick you mean?"

"No . . . not like that."

She lowered her eyes.

"Give me the money," he said.

"I don't have it in cash," she said quietly. "We'll have to go to the bank. I'll go get dressed."

"I'll give it back," he said again, when she was ready. "You don't believe me. I want you to believe me."

"I want to," she said. "I want to believe you."

Her bank was a Chemical branch on Sheridan Square. He didn't go in with her. He waited outside, on Seventh Avenue, by the curb. When she gave him the money, he crumpled the bills in his fist and put his arms tightly around her. She could feel him pressing hard against her — his fisted hand, nestled in the hollow between her shoulder blades, pressing hardest. Her own arms were down. She didn't have the fortitude to hold him, knowing she couldn't stop him from going.

Neither she nor he said good-bye.

He walked away, and she watched him weave his way amidst the people on the street till he turned east on Bleecker.

The asphalt, the sidewalk pavement, people, parked and moving cars were suffused with radiant light. Beatrice continued to stare down the street. She knew she wouldn't see him again. As she was thinking this, she saw a brilliant light — light over light, like sudden glare — that made her feel a stunning awe and, underneath, numb joy. It came, went, and grief closed in.

Through tears the sun-drenched avenue looked like a tunnel of light with no reachable end. It was, they said, what one saw before dying.

As the taxi bringing Beatrice home came to a stop, Perkins was coming out of the building. He signaled to the driver to wait, took a step forward, then stood still, watching impassively as Beatrice crawled out of the car doubled over with pain, blood seeping like piss into the crotch and legs of her jeans.

He did not try to help her as she wobbled toward him.

He stepped aside to let her pass.

He followed her with his eyes as she staggered to the stairway and fell, hitting her forehead on the edge of the first step.

He signaled to the driver again to wait. He turned around and walked back into the building. He hesitated a long moment before picking her up in his arms.

He looked down at her limp body, her eyes, rolled up, only the whites showing.

He said: "Can you hear me?"

He said: "Do you know who I am?"

He said: "What's my name?"

He carried her out.

He waited for the taxi driver to open the car door.

He laid her down on the backseat, sliding his arms from under her carefully, slowly, then shut the door and stepped back.

He turned his hands over and stared at the blood on his palms.

He said to the taxi driver: "Go!"

He kept his eyes on the car as it moved down the street, standing with his arms at a slight bias to his hips, palms facing outward, so as not to stain his pants.

◈

After the D and C, they kept her in the hospital overnight. She was released the next day, in the afternoon.

She left in her bloodied clothes.

She came home. She took a shower. She toweled herself dry. She put on a denim skirt and a bright red sweater. She did not put shoes on. She took a comb and dug the teeth deep into her scalp. She passed the comb through her wet hair, pulling it through the tangles harder and harder, till tears came to her eyes. She threw the comb across the room. She walked to the kitchen and opened the cupboard where the liquor was kept. She took out a pint of Myers rum. She sat on the couch, holding the bottle in her lap. She uncapped the bottle and brought it to her lips. She tried to sip but couldn't swallow. She put the bottle, uncapped, down on the coffee table. She sat deeper in the couch with her back straight against the bolster. She sat completely still.

She felt a wholeness in herself that was completely empty — as though there was no before in her life, as though everything and everyone she'd lost had been no real part of her and what was left — what was still there — had always been there and could never be destroyed. That, she thought, *that* was her — this knowledge of permanence and strength.

The early spring light coming through the windows filled the loft with equal brightness wall to wall. The air was alive with light. The cleared space was full of light, its emptiness a hollow word. She was surrounded by light. All was light, and it was a clear sharp light such as did not shine on dreams.

Before — everything before — had been like a dream, had vanished like a dream. From all of it, only Perkins remained. She could hear him pacing, a jarring sound.

Can you hear me? What's my name?

Do you know who I am?

No, she didn't know who he was: he'd touched her — he had tried to help her.

She went to bed at the first darkening of dusk. She lay on her side. She curled her legs up to her chest. She smelled Chris's scent on the pillow and felt a tingling quiver between her legs. She laid her hand where his body had lain and cried herself to sleep.

She woke up at midnight to pitch black and the raucous sound of laughter and voices from Colin's loft. Through it, softer, came stereo music — the Velvet Underground, Lou Reed singing:

> *Over the bridge we go*
> *Looking for love*

The floorboards vibrated from the bass beat, and as she walked fumbling in the dark to find the light switch on the wall, the music thumped into her naked feet, making her feel like she was airborne in the dark, the song pulsing through her, a soul-tremor in her blood.

> *Something's got a hold on me*
> *And I don't know what . . .*
> *It's the beginning of a new age*
> *It's a new age*

The music momentarily stopped, then played again on the same track.

Beatrice stood with her hand on the switch, afraid to turn on the light. One click, one flick of her finger, and there it would be — the rest of her life.

A NOTE ABOUT THE AUTHOR

Irini Spanidou is the author of the novels *God's Snake* and *Fear*. She lives in New York City.

A NOTE ON THE TYPE

The text of this book was set in Electra, a typeface designed
by W. A. Dwiggins (1880–1956). This face cannot be classi-
fied as either modern or old style. It is not based on any his-
torical model, nor does it echo any particular period or style.

Composed by Stratford/TexTech,
Brattleboro, Vermont
Printed and bound by R. R. Donnelley & Sons,
Harrisonburg, Virginia
Design by Wesley Gott